The Ornament Tree

"It must be an old tree with branches that curve, like embracing arms," Cousin Audra explained. "When we want to honor someone we love, or remember someone who has gone away, we write the person's name on a strip of paper and tie it to a branch. Others write down the things that worry them, and when the paper blows away, the worries go with it. We never look at anyone else's strip."

"The next-door neighbor says it's a witch's tree," Clare offered with a grin. "But we think she's crazy. Of course, she thinks the same about us."

There was a small silence and then Carson Younger threw back his head and shouted with laughter.

"Well now, Miss Bonnie Shaster," he said. "You have found yourself in interesting company, haven't you?"

Other Avon Flare Books by
Jean Thesman

CATTAIL MOON
MOLLY DONNELLY
RACHEL CHANCE
THE RAIN CATCHERS
THE WHITNEY COUSINS: HEATHER

Avon Camelot Books

WHEN THE ROAD ENDS

Coming Soon in Avon Flare

THE ELLIOTT COUSINS:
  (1) JAMIE
  (2) MEREDITH
  (3) TERESA

The Ornament Tree

JEAN THESMAN

AN AVON FLARE BOOK

AVON BOOKS
A division of
The Hearst Corporation
1350 Avenue of the Americas
New York, New York 10019

Copyright © 1996 by Jean Thesman
Published by arrangement with Houghton Mifflin Company
Visit our website at **http://www.AvonBooks.com**
Library of Congress Catalog Card Number: 95-17102
ISBN: 0-380-72912-1

First Avon Flare Printing: March 1998

AVON FLARE TRADEMARK REG. U.S. PAT. OFF. AND IN OTHER COUNTRIES, MARCA REGISTRADA, HECHO EN U.S.A.

Printed in the U.S.A.

WCD   10   9   8   7   6   5   4   3   2   1

*This is for the real Clare and her sister
who told me the stories, which were always
more loving and comic than I could ever echo.*

*Also, this is for Mr. Younger, misplaced in time
and circumstances but never in Clare's affection.*

1

Dear Elena:

I haven't heard from you since I came here to live
with Aunt Suze, and I'm worried. I hope you and
your family are well.

Is Los Angeles still as exciting to you as it was
when you first moved there? Did your father find
work at the motion picture studio? Is your brother
feeling better now? Please forgive all the questions,
but it's been so long since you wrote.

At last I'm escaping from this place. As I told
you before, I promised Aunt Suze I would stay for
the summer to pay her back for helping me arrange
Mama's funeral and sell the farm. But I'm leaving
today for Seattle, where I'll live with Mama's people in the house where she grew up.

It seems like years since we did our homework
together in the back room of your father's shop.
Who could have dreamed that he would lose his

business and my mother would pass away so suddenly?

Please write to me at the address below. I'm worried about you. Give your family my love.

Sincerely,
Bonnie

"You'll regret this, Bonnie. You'll be sorry."

Bonnie looked up briefly at Aunt Suze, and then bent over her suitcase again. Her torrent of curly blond hair fell around her face, hiding her trembling mouth. I won't let her make me cry this time, she told herself. But if Aunt Suze would only *get out* of her bedroom and let her finish packing!

Aunt Suze leaned her bulky shoulder against the door and folded her hands under her stained apron. "You ought to be ashamed, after everything Don and me done for you since your ma died. It's not cheap these days, feeding an extra kid."

"The lawyer paid you for my board and room," Bonnie said. "He told me that." She folded a summer cotton petticoat and jammed it into the suitcase. "And I worked. All summer long I worked for you. Now I'm going to Mama's family in Seattle, and I'll go on to college, just as she planned for me."

"Plans have to be changed sometimes," Aunt Suze said. She was wearing the self-satisfied expression Bonnie had come to dread. "None of us ever gets to do everything we want. We have to make sacrifices. You've had more schooling than I ever did, and there's nobody who can say that I don't get along just fine and better than most. What can a fancy private school do for you? And college? You'll end up married, with a house full of kids to take care of."

But I won't be on a farm, Bonnie thought bitterly. The farm is what killed Mama.

But even as she thought it, she knew it wasn't exactly true. Mama died of typhoid fever. But maybe she could have fought it off if she hadn't been so tired. If Papa had still been alive. If the hired man hadn't left for better money in the next town. If the doctor had put her in the hospital in time.

Bonnie folded her second-best blouse carefully, set it on top of the other clothes in the old straw suitcase, and then closed the lid. Behind her on the floor, her trunk had already been filled with everything else she owned. In less than half an hour, Mr. Joshua, her mother's lawyer, would take her to the train depot. Late tomorrow afternoon she would be in Seattle, in Cousin Audra's house, and the hot, bitter summer of 1918 would be only a bad memory.

"That Audra Devereaux, she'll put you to work, all right," Aunt Suze said. "I know her kind. You think she'll treat you like her own granddaughter, but you'd better think again. You'll be a maid to her and hers, and maybe you'll go to school for a while, but it won't do you any good, because she'll never let you go to college. You're fourteen now. Audra won't put up with you keeping your nose in a book when there's work to be done. You'll see. You'll be back here before the harvest's over, begging us to take you in again."

Never, Bonnie thought. Never! She bent to see herself in the watery mirror over her dresser. Hair a mess, skin sunburned and freckled. She brushed her hair and secured it at the back of her neck with a short length of narrow black ribbon.

Outside, the dogs erupted into barks and howls, and Aunt Suze's boys shrieked wildly.

"Mr. Joshua must be here," Bonnie said. She picked

up her pocketbook and the suitcase and started for the door. Aunt Suze stepped aside, scowling.

"Maybe the boys could help with my trunk," Bonnie said. "Please," she added.

"Maybe not," Aunt Suze said.

Bonnie's chin went up. All right, she thought. Let it end this way, then. She hurried down the steps to the front door. This part of my life is almost over. I can afford to smile.

The front door stood open, and old Mr. Joshua saw her as he climbed the front porch steps. "All ready, are you?" he asked.

"All ready," she said. She set her suitcase down on the porch. "I've got a trunk upstairs, but I don't think I can get it down by myself. Is Harry with you?"

Harry was the handyman who drove the auto for Mr. Joshua most of the time. Bonnie had been counting on his help at the depot, but it seemed that she needed it now, too. Junior and G. G. were running wild with the dogs in the side yard, and they wouldn't help unless their mother insisted.

"I'm by myself," Mr. Joshua said. "But I can get the trunk for you. Just point the way."

He was too old and fragile to drag the trunk downstairs. "You take my suitcase out to the auto," she said. "I'll manage the trunk."

She ran upstairs and caught Aunt Suze at the window, staring down at the shining automobile. Without a word, Bonnie grabbed one handle and skidded the trunk over the rough pine floor.

"Take care you don't scratch that floor," Aunt Suze snapped. "You'll have to pay to fix it."

"Then help me with the trunk," Bonnie said.

Aunt Suze opened her mouth, then shut it again. "Mind your feet," she said as she grabbed the other handle and slid the trunk around, barely missing Bonnie's shoes.

They got the trunk downstairs, but not without Aunt Suze's unending complaints. Mr. Joshua helped shove it into the back of the auto and slammed the door on it.

"So, Suze," he said, eyeing Aunt Suze critically. "I saw how good your wheat looks when I drove up the road. Best I've seen in the whole county. You've had a fine year."

"Not fine enough, Don says," Aunt Suze said.

Mr. Joshua looked out over the fields and tapped his chin with a gnarled forefinger. Aunt Suze stared with unblinking resentment at his fine auto.

"You sent that telegram to Seattle, didn't you, Suze?" Mr. Joshua asked suddenly.

Bonnie gasped and turned to stare at Aunt Suze. She had asked her aunt and uncle to send a telegram to Seattle for her the last time they went to town. She wanted Cousin Audra to know her arrival time, so she had written the message carefully and given them more than enough money to pay for it.

"You sent it?" she asked her aunt.

"A'course I did," Aunt Suze said. Two bright red spots appeared on her weathered cheeks—and Bonnie knew she lied.

"Of course you did," Mr. Joshua said soothingly. His white eyebrows lifted innocently over his clear blue eyes. "Of *course* you did. But no matter if you did or you didn't, I'm going to send another one when we get to town, just to make sure Bonnie's people know she's on her way at last."

"*We're* Bonnie's people," Aunt Suze said. "We're the ones she owes."

"She owes nothing to nobody. You're her father's stepsister, and that's not blood kin and you know it, so

5

don't you go heaping blame on this child at the last minute," Mr. Joshua said.

"There's things that matter more than being blood kin," Aunt Suze said.

"And I'm thinking you might not know the first thing about any of them," Mr. Joshua said. "Mind you, I'll be back here Monday a week to pick up your accounts, because it's time I showed the judge how you've been spending Bonnie's allowance these last three months."

"Maybe you better pay attention to how Audra Devereaux will spend Bonnie's money," Aunt Suze snapped.

Mr. Joshua smiled. "I remember Audra Devereaux," he said. He savored her name, as if it had a delicate, delicious flavor. "I remember her gray eyes. Like Bonnie's eyes, they were. And like her mama's."

Aunt Suze backed inside the door and slammed it. Mr. Joshua laughed. "Get aboard, child," he said. "It's a long hot drive to the depot."

Aunt Suze's boys circled the auto, shrieking, until their father came out of the barn to yell at them. Bonnie told him good-bye, but Don didn't answer, and only went back into the barn as if he hadn't heard or seen anything out of the ordinary. The boys' farewell consisted of shrill demands for money and rides in the auto, both of which Mr. Joshua refused with short, barking curses and, once, an open-handed slap at the oldest boy's behind. The blow missed, and the boy's piercing laughter brought on more barking and yapping from the dogs.

"Those boys will see the inside of a jail before they ever see a paycheck," Mr. Joshua said as the auto bumped down the driveway to the road. "Well, you won't have to put up with them anymore, Bonnie."

"You know Audra Devereaux?" she asked.

"No, no, but I saw a miniature of her once," Mr.

Joshua said. He honked the auto horn at a cow wandering along the side of the road. The cow stopped to stare, then lumbered into the ditch to escape. A young girl darted out through a break in a wire fence, shouting at the cow.

"Your mama showed that miniature to me," Mr. Joshua went on. "I never forgot it. I never got over it, either. Audra had hair like white gold and big gray eyes. My, my, it was love at first sight, and me only sixty-three at the time, too."

Bonnie laughed. "I have the miniature in my trunk," she said. "I've looked at it every night since Mama died."

Mr. Joshua reached out a hand and squeezed her arm. "You'll love Seattle, and from everything I've heard about your mama's cousin, you'll love her, too. She won't let you feel like a stranger."

It was too much to hope for, but Bonnie hoped, anyway.

She looked out across the ripened wheat, bending and rippling under the pale wind-blown sky and marveled that the great plain could seem so beautiful now, and so terrifying in December, in a blizzard.

"It rains all the time in Seattle, doesn't it?" she asked the old man.

"Rain, fog, snow, sunshine," he said. "You'll get it all."

She smiled and hugged her thin arms across her chest.

The train rattled west into the flaming sunset, through mountain passes in the moonlit dark, and then through deep green valleys veiled in morning mists. *Never go back, never go back*, the train wheels said.

She had never seen the place where she was going, and she had never met the women with whom she would

7

be living. Sometimes, when she let herself think about it, the strangeness of it all frightened her. There had been times during the past weeks when she had almost lost her courage. But she remembered all the things her mother had told her about the Seattle cousins and the life she would lead there, and so she pushed on toward the goal.

Mama, she thought, soon I'll see the city where you grew up. The train depot in Seattle was hot, gritty, and crowded with soldiers. Everyone said the Great War was nearly over, so Bonnie wondered where they had come from and where they were going. They brushed past her with scarcely a glance, and after they left, another train disgorged another crowd, this time of tired, soot-smeared families. Some were met by people they knew, and others hurried away as if they knew exactly where they were going.

Bonnie found a bench on the platform and sat down, with her suitcase by her feet. She was desperately tired, for she hadn't been able to sleep sitting up on the train, and her head had begun to ache.

Where could Cousin Audra be? She had promised she would be waiting.

Bonnie brushed at the soot on her jacket and tried to tidy her hair. Wouldn't Aunt Suze laugh if she saw me now, Bonnie thought. I look like something the cat dragged in, and nobody's here to meet me, and I'm so hungry I could cry!

From the bench, she saw the longer hand on the great clock on the wall click forward, marking the passing time. She searched the crowd, looking for a woman with pale hair who would be looking for her. A half hour passed, then another fifteen minutes after that.

Don't worry, she told herself. Soon Cousin Audra will come, and I'll go where Mama and I should have moved three years ago, when Papa died. I'll stay in Mama's old bedroom and go to her old school with Audra's grand-daughter, and everything will be just as Mama wanted it to be.

Bonnie's headache was almost unbearable. She got to her feet unsteadily, biting her lip to keep from crying. She must have something to eat and a strong cup of tea, and then she would find Cousin Audra's house. There was a lunch counter inside the building, and she made her way to it.

A short, fat man in a tight gray coat stepped up to her, his thick lips pulled into a smile. "Looking for somebody, miss?"

"What?" He had startled Bonnie, and it took her a few seconds to focus on what he had said.

The man pulled off a soiled derby and held it to his chest. "I been watching you, and you seem to be in trouble, miss. Looking for somebody? Don't have any-place to go? Is there some way I can help you?"

Bonnie drew back a little, but she didn't want to seem rude, so she said, "No, thank you. I'll be fine."

"A nice young lady like yourself won't be fine for very long in a train station, not unless somebody's meet-ing her. Is somebody meeting you here?"

Bonnie longed to burst into tears and tell the stranger how tired she was and how she seemed to have missed Cousin Audra, but she knew better. She picked up her suitcase and said, "I don't need help, but thank you any-way."

He followed her inside the building, scarcely half a step behind. "Heading for the lunch counter? I need a cup of coffee myself. I'm waiting for my sister, and her train's late. I'm the desk clerk at a nice little hotel a few blocks from here and Agatha—she's my sister—is com-ing to work there with me. We're always looking for good, honest maids and kitchen help. If it's a job you need, you can't do better than that little hotel. Why looky there—I see two empty places at the counter. Let's sit down before we fall down, and I'll tell you about that job and the nice room that goes with it.''

Bonnie knew she shouldn't, but when the man gently took her arm, holding it above the elbow, and steered her toward the lunch counter, she went without protest.

2

The moment she sat down, the man behind the counter abandoned another customer, who was ordering from a fly-specked menu, and grabbed a sopping gray rag.

"What'll it be, miss?" he asked as he swabbed the counter in front of her, pushing a puddle of dirty water ahead of the rag. Even though he spoke to her, his angry gaze was on the fat little man in the gray coat.

"Tea, please," Bonnie said.

"And I'll have coffee, and maybe a slice of—" the man in the gray coat began.

"You'll have *nothing*," the man behind the counter said. "I told you before to carry on your filthy business someplace else."

The man in the gray coat drew himself up straight. "How dare you, sir. This is a free country—"

The man behind the counter flapped the rag suddenly, splattering water on the other man. "Beat it or I'll get the cops in here," he said quietly.

The man in the gray coat scuttled away, brushing at the wet spots on his coat, muttering furiously to himself.

"Miss," the man behind the counter said, "I don't know who you are or where you came from, but don't

11

ever take up with a stranger in a train station. Understand what I'm saying to you? That Mike, did he tell you he might have a job for you?''

Bonnie's lips were numb with shock. "Something like that. He said he was waiting for his sister, and she was going to work at a hotel, but I don't—"

"Sister, my eye," the man behind the counter said disgustedly. "I'll get you a cup of tea, because you look like you need it. But when you're done, you get out of this place."

The tea, when it came, was black and bitter, and she couldn't drink it. She paid the counter man and left.

Her suitcase seemed heavier than before. Her dark blue traveling suit was grimy with soot and heavily wrinkled. Her hair had come loose from the ribbon and was tangled around her face.

She walked across the great, crowded depot, heading back toward the platform and her trunk, but she saw with amazement that someone was holding up a sign bearing her own name, Bonnie Shaster. An elderly woman whose dark gray-streaked hair was cut short in the newest style searched the crowd around her.

That can't be Cousin Audra, Bonnie thought. But she couldn't stop the smile that spread over her face as she hurried forward. What did it matter who this woman was? She was looking specifically for Bonnie Shaster, and since she knew her name, she must be safe.

"I'm Bonnie," she said when she got close to the woman, who was looking everywhere except at her.

"Heavens!" the woman exclaimed. "Did you jump off that train while it was still moving? I didn't expect to see you come in yet, so you caught me by surprise. The train was on time? Trains are never on time. But here you are, and aren't you the sweetest thing? Is that suitcase all you've got?"

"I was afraid you weren't coming!" Bonnie blurted. "I've been here since four o'clock."

"But the telegram said you were arriving at five," the woman cried vexedly. "Dear girl, you've been waiting all this time? Drat those telegraph people. They're always making mistakes. You must have thought we'd forgotten about you."

Bonnie blinked back tears. "I *was* getting worried," she admitted.

"Well, heavens, why not?" the woman said. "I worry when someone's five minutes late. Don't you have a trunk? No matter, we'll get you what you need."

"I've got a trunk, out on the platform," Bonnie said.

"Come along and we'll find somebody to take charge of it," the woman said. She folded the cardboard sign bearing Bonnie's name and shoved it into a trash can, then snatched up the suitcase as if it weighed next to nothing.

Bonnie ran after the woman as she strode through the door leading to the platforms. Her skirt was inches above her ankles, and her gray stockings were silk. She was the only elderly woman Bonnie had ever seen whose skirt didn't touch her shoe tops.

But who was she?

Bonnie pointed out her trunk, and the woman immediately waved to a rumpled man in dirty clothes who had been leaning against a post, gnawing on a matchstick, and watching people pass.

"You there, we'll need this trunk delivered," the woman said. She pulled a sheet of paper from her pocketbook and scribbled the address while the man stared. "Here's a dollar to start you out," the woman told the gawking man. "You'll get another when you bring the trunk." She shoved the paper and the silver dollar at him.

13

The man nodded and smiled at her, showing broken teeth and gaps. "I can't read," he admitted cheerfully, handing back the paper. "You tell me the address and I'll remember it, missus."

"Oh, stars and bars," the woman muttered. She rattled off an address. "Can I count on you?"

"Like death and taxes," the man said. He repeated the address back to her, and then asked for her name.

"I'm Winnie Devereaux," the woman said. "If you get lost, just ask for directions to the Devereaux house on Crescent Road. Everybody in the neighborhood knows us. They might not be speaking to us, but they know us."

Winnie Devereaux was another cousin, Bonnie remembered. She had lived with Cousin Audra for many years, along with Audra's daughter, Sally, and Sally's twelve-year-old daughter, Clare. And now, Bonnie Shaster would also live in the Devereaux house on Crescent Road. She hadn't been forgotten after all.

"I can take the suitcase, too, missus," the man said, and Winnie handed it to him. "We're trusting you," she told him.

"And you're right to trust me," the man said proudly.

Winnie watched him shamble off with the suitcase, and satisfied with what she saw, she said, "There. That's taken care of. Now let's get you home. The place is a madhouse this afternoon, which is why Audra couldn't come. The telegram surprised us, not that you aren't more welcome than good luck and Christmas both, but our newest boarder arrives today, and settling him in will be complicated. He was blinded in the war, poor soul, and his mother's bringing him. She'll want dinner with us to make sure we're going to feed him well, and she's spending the night, too. And Mrs. Marshall, she's our housekeeper, is threatening revolution. She says she

14

won't cook for our boarders unless we hire her niece to help all day every day, but the girl's worse than useless.''

Bonnie, running beside Winnie, was losing track of the conversation. "Boarders?" she asked. She didn't know Cousin Audra took in boarders. Why would she? She was rich.

"Four of 'em," Winnie said. "Here, we can take this streetcar."

"Four boarders?" Bonnie asked.

"Four gentlemen, boarders and roomers," Winnie said. They climbed the streetcar steps and Winnie dropped their fares through the slot in the glass box.

"Sit here, darling girl," she said as she pointed toward a bench seat on the shady side of the car. "We don't have far to go. Yes, we have four gentlemen. Audra and I wanted to take in women, don't you know, but Mr. Grimsley from the bank said women don't have any money, and isn't that God's truth? Why else would we need to take in boarders? He said he'd find four gentlemen who want a good address and respectable surroundings, and he has. But this business is new to us, and we keep running into complications. Nobody paid the iceman so he wouldn't leave a block the day before yesterday, and barely an hour ago Mrs. Marshall says the beef might have gone off. Now how will that look to the new boarder's mother? You can see why Audra had to stay behind and manage things."

Bonnie's ears rang. She had never known anyone who talked so much, and while the story was entertaining, it was also alarming. If Cousin Audra had fallen on hard times and had to take in boarders, would she want another person to feed? Mr. Joshua would pay an allowance to Cousin Audra out of Mama's estate for Bonnie's board and room, just as he had to Aunt Suze, but Bonnie was well aware of how much a family could resent an extra and unwanted person in the household.

I'll work hard to make myself useful to Cousin Audra, she resolved. But oh, if things could only have been different! If only nothing had changed from the time Mama and her widowed mother had moved in with Cousin Audra, then just a young bride.

Boarders! What would Mama have thought of that?

The streetcar rattled through town, along a busy street between the tallest buildings Bonnie had ever seen. Mr. Joshua's automobile was an exciting curiosity to his neighbors in the farm community. Here in Seattle, automobiles were everywhere. Between buildings on the west, she caught glimpses of Puget Sound, great ships at the docks, and distant green islands. The sight of so much water dazzled her. The streetcar clanged and followed tracks around a corner, then up a steep hill, leaving the business district behind. It bustled down tree-lined streets where children played on sidewalks and ladies in white dresses sat back in the shadows on deep porches.

"Here we are," Winnie said briskly as she got to her feet. "Heavens, will you look at that?"

Bonnie followed her off the streetcar and saw a wagon filled with blocks of ice nestled in straw, stopped at the curb before a large white house. A stout man wearing a leather shield over one shoulder confronted a thin girl who stood in the wagon bed, while another girl fled down the block, her red hair bouncing on her shoulders.

"Thief!" the man shouted at the girl in the wagon.

"Who are you calling thief!" Winnie cried as she started across the street. "Clare, get out of that wagon this instant, and put down your skirt!"

The brown-haired girl had been holding her skirt so high above her knees that her garters showed, and she

16

dropped it now. Bonnie saw chips of ice stuck to it. It was obvious that the girl, Clare, had been stealing ice chips, and Bonnie would have laughed at the sight, but the man's next words appalled her.

"Miss Sneak Thief Clare Harris owes me five cents for the ice chips she stole," the man bellowed. "And somebody in this house owes me one dollar and forty cents for all the ice I've carried here this summer, and I want my money right now!"

"How dare you stand out here in the street and shout!" Winnie cried. She darted toward the man's horse and smacked its flank with her pocketbook. "Git, Rosamund. You git!"

Fat Rosamund turned her head and observed Winnie with a calm, dark eye. She shifted her feet obligingly, but didn't move an inch.

"I want money!" the man howled.

"I'll pay you if you stop bellowing," Winnie said. She groped through her pocket book and took out a handful of change. "I have—let's see—I have eighty-five cents here. You take it and get out of here, but not before you take a block of ice around back and put it in the icebox."

"No ice until I get a dollar and forty cents, and five cents more from Miss Sneak Thief Clare," the man shouted.

Clare jumped down from the wagon bed and marched toward the front porch, her fair skin scarlet, her chin raised stubbornly. "Ice chips aren't worth *anything*!" she said.

"Five cents!" roared the man.

"Here, here's the rest of your money," Bonnie said, and she pulled her coin purse out of her pocket. She gave him sixty cents while Winnie protested. "Now where's the ice?" Bonnie asked sharply.

"Another Miss Smartypants!" the man grumbled. "Another Miss Smartypants heard from." He sank his tongs into a block of ice and hoisted it to his shoulder. "There's too many women in this house," he complained to Rosamund as he passed her.

"Lord!" Winnie fumed. "What next? I hope I'm wrong, but I think our new boarder is here."

A small thin woman and a tall young man approached the house slowly, reluctantly. The woman held the young man's arm. He wore glasses with black lenses and he touched the sidewalk carefully with a cane. The blind boarder had arrived.

The woman nodded to Winnie and glanced apprehensively at the iceman, who was storming through the side gate with his burden and muttering darkly to himself.

"Stars and bars," Winnie murmured.

"Indeed," the young man said as he turned his lean face toward her. "Indeed, madam. I hope this is not the boarding house."

"It is," Winnie said. "We're having a difficult day. The iceman, well, what can I say? And I've just come back from the depot with Bonnie, and—"

The man stumbled a little on a section of sidewalk forced out of place by the roots of a giant maple tree. The woman gasped and clutched at his arm, and he shook her off impatiently. "I can do it, Mother," he said, and he strode forward and stumbled again.

Bonnie reached out and steadied him before he could fall. "Look out," she cautioned, and then she burst into embarrassed tears at her tactless words.

"What have we here?" the young man asked. He raised one hand and his seeking fingers touched her hair. "You're Bonnie, are you, with all this wild hair? I trust you have nothing whatever to do with stolen ice and boarding houses."

18

"But I do," Bonnie said. She stepped back from him and rubbed her tears away on the backs of her hands. "I'll be living here, too," she said.

"Ah," the young man said, and he grinned suddenly. "Well, come along, Mother. I'd like to know more about this establishment."

The iceman passed on his way back to his wagon. "This house is run by *women!*" he shouted. "They pass out pamphlets on street corners. *Votes* for Women! And worse! Shameful pamphlets about things decent ladies don't know anything about!" He pulled himself up into the wagon seat and mopped his face with a dirty handkerchief. "Git, Rosamund. Git."

The horse cast one last appraising look at the people on the sidewalk, and then leaned into her harness and pulled. Bonnie could have sworn that she smiled.

What have I gotten myself into? Bonnie thought.

At that moment, a small woman with white-blond braids wound around her head stepped out on the porch. This was Cousin Audra, Bonnie knew. She was older than she had been when her miniature had been painted, but she could have posed for it that afternoon.

"Is that you, Bonnie?" she called. "Clare said you were here." She hurried down the steps, embraced Bonnie, and kissed both her cheeks. Then she turned to the woman and her blind son. "You must be Mrs. Younger, of course, and this is your son, Carson." She took each one by the hand. "I'm Audra Devereaux. I can't tell you how glad I am to see you. Come along. We're about to have a late tea, out here in the shade on the side porch, and you're just in time."

Cousin Audra had mended the frightful, hot afternoon. Smiling, speaking softly in her sweet voice, she led the three newcomers to the side porch and seated them in cushioned wicker chairs.

"Winnie and I will be back right away with tea," she said. The screen door shut quietly behind her.

Late summer roses grew over the porch and scented the air. Bonnie took a deep breath, and for the first time, she dared to relax.

"What does she look like?" the young man asked his mother.

"Mrs. Devereaux?" she asked. "She's, well, I don't know, son. She's small, and she has beautiful hair, blond mixed with gray, braided into a crown, and her eyes are gray."

"Ah," Carson Younger said. He leaned back in his chair. "And what do you look like, Bonnie?"

Bonnie stared at him. "I don't know," she said hesitantly. This is how he learns about people, she thought. He didn't mean to be rude.

"She looks a little like Mrs. Devereaux, only younger," Mrs. Younger said. "And her hair is curly."

"Ah," Carson Younger said. He turned toward Bonnie and asked, "Where have you been?"

"Been?" she asked.

"The other lady said she had to get you at the depot. Where have you been?"

"I was home," Bonnie said. "Well, this is my home now. I've only just arrived here, at my new home."

"A boarding house, with pamphlet ladies and someone named Clare who steals ice. How old are you, Bonnie?"

"Fourteen," she said.

"Run for your life," he said, and he laughed.

3

❦❦❦❦

After a few minutes, Audra and Winnie brought peppermint tea in thin china cups. A moment later, a freckled woman with bobbed hair appeared in the doorway with a plate of lemon cookies.

Clare followed, wearing a clean white apron over her damp dress, and carrying thick embroidered linen napkins. Her brown braids had been slicked down with water, and her mouth was set defiantly as she stared at Bonnie.

Bonnie accepted her tea and a cookie, and smiled at Clare when the girl handed her a napkin. There was no point in giving Clare the idea that she felt superior in any way just because she had witnessed the scene with the iceman. But Clare wasn't appeased by the smile, and she stalked away to her own chair without changing her haughty expression.

Audra introduced her family to the Youngers in a charming way, saying, "Mrs. Younger, Mr. Younger, please let me present my daughter, Sally Harris, who is the head librarian at our local branch." The freckled woman smiled and nodded.

"And," Audra went on, "here is her daughter, our

21

Clare, who attends Miss Delaney's Academy for Young Ladies.''

Clare glared up at them from under her straight eyebrows and nodded briefly.

Audra went on as if she hadn't noticed. "Mrs. Younger, you've already met Winnie Devereaux, my late husband's cousin. Winnie is president of the local chapter of the Women's Citizens Committee, and she works with me at the South Neighborhood House."

Mrs. Younger smiled at this and said, "How d'you do, Miss Devereaux. I'm involved with the same sort of work in Portland. I hope we'll have a chance to talk before I return."

"Next," Audra said, "is our newest family member, our darling cousin, Bonnie Shaster, who has come to us to prepare for college."

Mr. Younger's head was cocked to one side as he listened attentively. Bonnie thought that he, too, enjoyed the way Audra introduced everyone. Now there would be none of the awkwardness that usually came with meeting strangers, for everyone knew a little something about everyone else, and could ask questions or make comments. Mrs. Younger had already taken advantage of what she knew of Winnie.

The adults murmured to one another comfortably, while a late afternoon breeze trembled in the vines that grew over the porch and carried with it the scent of roses and freshly cut grass. Clare ate one cookie and drank half a cup of tea, then stared at her feet. Bonnie, famished, finished her tea and two cookies quickly. She tried not to glance at Clare, but she couldn't stop herself. Clare obviously was not prepared to make friends easily.

She doesn't want me here, Bonnie thought. It's more than just getting caught stealing when I was watching and then being yelled at by that awful man. She doesn't like me.

Mr. Younger sipped his tea but refused cookies. When he cocked his head while he listened, Bonnie knew that he had heard something that interested him particularly. But most of the time, he seemed remote and shut off, trapped inside his own thoughts.

A horse and rundown wagon stopped in front, and the man from the depot jumped out of the back. He had brought Bonnie's trunk and suitcase, just as he promised. Winnie dashed inside and came back a moment later with another silver dollar. The man put the baggage inside the door and shuffled away, smiling, flipping the dollar into the air. The wagon driver chirped to the horse, and the wagon rumbled off, while the people on the porch watched in lazy, relaxed silence. Bees hummed in the vines.

"Where is your baggage, Mr. Younger?" Audra asked, rousing herself from her contemplation of leaf shadows dancing on the wall of the house. "May we send somewhere for it?"

"I made arrangements at the dock," Mrs. Younger said. "They promised it would be here before dark."

"You came to Seattle on a boat?" Clare asked, surprising them all with her sudden interest.

"Yes, from Portland," Mrs. Younger said. "I don't care for train travel, and Carson obliged me by putting up with a short voyage."

"This time of year the weather on the coast is wonderful," Winnie said. "The voyage might have been uncomfortable later in the year."

"Only the worst weather in the world for sailing," Sally said. "I hate the trip myself."

Carson Younger wasn't listening to them. "I hear paper fluttering in the wind somewhere," he said.

Audra laughed. "How observant of you. It's the Ornament Tree, out here in the side yard."

"Heavens above," Mrs. Younger said. "I haven't heard of an Ornament Tree since my grandmother died years ago. I didn't know anyone believed in them any longer."

"We have a fine old apple tree we've appointed to be our Ornament Tree," Winnie said. "But Audra and Clare are the only ones who tie paper strips to it. I'm afraid the rest of us have become too modern."

"What is an Ornament Tree?" Carson Younger asked.

Audra set her cup and saucer on the small wicker table next to her. "It must be an old tree with branches that curve, like embracing arms. When we want to honor someone we love very much, or remember someone who has gone away, we write the person's name on a small strip of paper and tie it to a branch."

"My grandmother wrote down the things that worried her," Mrs. Younger said, laughing a little. "She believed that when the paper fell apart and blew away, so would her troubles."

Carson Younger leaned forward. "And what is tied to your Ornament Tree, Mrs. Devereaux?"

"Carson!" his mother said. "That's their private business."

"Yes," Audra said. "We never look at anyone else's strip."

"The next-door neighbor says it's a witch's tree," Clare offered with a grin that showed white, even teeth. "But we think she's crazy. Of course, she thinks the same about us."

There was a small silence, and then Carson Younger threw back his head and shouted with laughter.

"Well, now, Miss Bonnie Shaster," he said. "You

have found yourself in interesting company, haven't you?''

Bonnie's face burned with a blush. ''I don't see anything wrong with an Ornament Tree. Mama told me about the one Cousin Audra has in her yard.''

''Carson is sometimes too blunt,'' Mrs. Younger said, quiet and resigned. ''Please excuse him.''

''It's all right,'' Audra said quietly. ''I like to think we are interesting.'' She smiled calmly, and Bonnie, seeing that, leaned back again in her chair, relieved. ''We are imaginative,'' Audra went on. ''We think girls prosper when they are raised up to appreciate all sorts of different things.''

Bonnie glanced at Clare again, and that time caught her staring. She was not smiling. Bonnie swallowed the lump in her throat and looked away.

''Clare, if you and Bonnie are finished with your tea, why don't you take her upstairs and show her the room the two of you will be sharing?''

Clare leaped to her feet, said, ''Come on, then,'' and hurried through the door. Bonnie followed, picking up her suitcase as she passed it.

She had a home, but she wasn't certain how this would turn out. It was important that Clare be a friend, but so far, she was withholding even a simple welcome.

Oddly, Bonnie felt a hard pang of homesickness for Aunt Suze's farm. At least it was familiar, and she hadn't expected much ahead of time, since she had known Suze all her life and she didn't delude herself with fantasies about her. But unknown Cousin Audra had always been almost magical.

They climbed broad, carpeted stairs to the second floor, and then narrower bare stairs to the third floor.

''We'll share the old nursery,'' Clare said. ''I had a corner bedroom on the second floor until Grandmother began renting rooms. Those men have the four best bedrooms on the second floor. Grandmother and Mama share a big one in the back, under our room, and Winnie has a small one next to them." She opened a door and shoved it back against the wall. "Here we are."

The room was large, with a sloping ceiling and a row of windows that overlooked the city and Puget Sound. The floor was bare except for a few small braided rugs. Both beds were narrow, but Bonnie saw feather mattresses and heaps of pillows on them. Each bed had a quilt folded over the foot. Under the windows sat two desks and two bookcases. Two large mahogany wardrobes sat side by side near the door.

Bonnie looked around. "It's wonderful," she said.

"It's cold and damp in the nursery in winter," Clare said with obvious satisfaction at being able to pass on bad news. "The only heat we'll get comes from this grate on the floor. See? Heat from Mama's room comes up here. When the furnace was put in, nobody thought anyone would ever use this floor again, so the men didn't put pipes up here. We'll freeze in winter. You'll be sorry you came."

"Winters are cold where I came from," Bonnie said. "My water pitcher froze every night."

Clare stared haughtily. "We don't have water pitchers here. We have faucets in the bathrooms." She finished with a tight, triumphant smile, and sat down on one of the beds.

"I've seen a bathroom before," Bonnie blurted angrily. "My parents' house had a bathroom."

"I didn't know," Clare said. "Grandmother said you lived on a farm, and I wasn't sure if you had indoor plumbing."

Bonnie turned her back. "I guess this bed is mine," she said. She opened her suitcase on it. "I'm going to

26

bathe and change to clean clothes before dinner.''

"Certainly," Clare said. "I won't wait for you. Mrs. Marshall will call you for dinner." She left and the door clicked shut behind her.

Clare hates me, Bonnie thought. This won't work. What am I going to do? Where can I go?

She thought of the man in the depot who tried to interest her in working in a hotel, although the man at the lunch counter seemed to think something was wrong with that. Should she have let the hotel man explain what was available, just in case staying with Cousin Audra didn't work out and she needed a place to live and money to tide her over until she could contact Mr. Joshua and get his advice?

The dining room was large, paneled in dark wood, and carpeted from wall to wall. The table could easily seat twelve or more, and was set with a lace cloth and silver candlesticks. Scowling, Mrs. Marshall served roast beef, cold sliced ham, potato patties, and a variety of vegetables for dinner, along with hot biscuits, three kinds of jam, and crackers. Bonnie took second helpings of everything, but she ate in silence. She was too tired to speak, except to answer direct questions.

Mrs. Younger arranged her son's plate carefully, whispering, "The tomatoes are at twelve, the snap beans at three, the meat at six, and the potatoes at nine."

They pretend his plate is a clock, Bonnie thought. That way he can find everything.

Mrs. Younger cut his meat and buttered his biscuit, then served herself. Only Clare and Bonnie watched openly. The women busied themselves with their own meals and chatted with the other boarders, but Bonnie thought that Cousin Audra hadn't missed anything.

Mr. Malcom Partridge, an elderly lawyer, ate quickly,

taking small bites and sipping frequently from his water glass. He spoke in a low voice to Mr. Everett Nickerson, who had been introduced to Bonnie as an accountant for a department store. Mr. Nickerson was worried about his daughter, who had recently had a new baby and was not well.

One chair was empty. Winnie supplied the information that Mr. Bertram Johnson, a manager from the big shipyard, was having dinner downtown at one of the hotels. Bonnie and Mr. Younger would meet him tomorrow.

Halfway through the meal, Mrs. Marshall came in to tell Audra that Mr. Younger's trunk and several boxes had arrived. After much discussion, it was agreed that the delivery man should be paid extra to take Mr. Younger's belongings to his room and Bonnie's trunk to the third floor.

"You look exhausted, Bonnie," Audra said. "If you're finished with dinner, why don't you unpack and rest for a while? Clare can help."

"I'll help her," Winnie said as she got to her feet. "Bonnie and I are old friends by now."

Bonnie was relieved that Clare wouldn't be going up with her again. The girl's watchful, unblinking gaze was unnerving. As she climbed the steps with Winnie, she heard Audra ask Clare to play the piano for their guests.

Winnie helped her take her clothes from the trunk and put them away in the wardrobe. She smiled when she saw the miniature of Cousin Audra, and she set it on the bedside table. Bonnie stacked her books on the floor in front of one of the bookcases and said, "I can finish myself, Winnie."

"I know you can," Winnie said. "But a strange room's a lonely place. I thought I'd sit a while with you, and we can make some plans. The dressmaker is coming tomorrow for Clare's last fitting for her school uniforms. We'll have her measure you for your uniforms while she's here. She can take care of the rest of your clothes when there's more time. Clare already has her shoes and coat, so Audra will take you downtown tomorrow afternoon and outfit you."

"The lawyer said it would take two weeks or more to get money to Cousin Audra for my school things," Bonnie said, worrying.

"Stars, child," Winnie exclaimed. "Audra wouldn't dream of letting you buy your own clothes. What an idea! She buys everything for Clare, and pays her tuition, too. Why would she do less for you?"

"But you have to take in boarders—" Bonnie began. The conversation was embarrassing, as all conversations about money were.

"Ah, well," Winnie said, with a great sigh. "I'm afraid we haven't been good managers over the years. There are two mortgages on this house now, and six weeks ago Audra's banker told her that she couldn't spend money any longer because there wasn't anything left to spend." Winnie sat down on the rocker next to Bonnie's bed and leaned back. "Well, wasn't that a day, and coming so soon after your mother died? Audra was quite distraught. But Sally works and I have a little income from my father's estate. Now, with what our gentlemen pay, I'm sure we'll manage very well."

"Why didn't someone write and tell me that I shouldn't come?" Bonnie whispered, horrified at the story.

Winnie leaned forward. "What? How could we do that? We wanted you here. What an idea! Well, let me tell you, the banker wasn't a bit of help. 'Sell the house,' says he. 'Take what's left after the mortgages are paid and set yourselves up in a nice apartment.' Can you imagine? I'm the one who thought of taking in roomers, and our plans were to fill the place with congenial women. But I told you that, didn't I? But no sir, the banker wouldn't stand for it. 'It's men who have the money,' says he. So here we are, with a house full. Mr. Younger seems like a nice enough fellow, doesn't he?''

"How can he manage, being blind?" Bonnie asked, thinking of the steps.

"His mother says he's been blind for nearly a year and is quite handy now. But we'll help out any way we can." Winnie seemed quite certain there was nothing they couldn't manage.

"Why did he move to Seattle?" Bonnie said. "Couldn't he stay in Portland with his mother?"

"Ah, there's the question," Winnie said. "That wasn't explained, but Audra thinks perhaps he wants to get away from his family and be on his own. I should think their pity would be very difficult to bear."

"Can he work?"

"No, child. He can't work, but there's money in the family, so he needn't worry. He's not like some who've come home crippled or blind from the war and don't have family money or any way to earn their keep. We see them here and there in the city already, begging for nickels. It makes me sick!"

Bonnie shoved her books on the shelves. "What about the other roomers?"

"Malcom Partridge never married. He doesn't like the bother of keeping his own house. And he can walk to his office from here. Mr. Everett Nickerson is a widower—we knew his wife—and he doesn't want to live with his daughter, now that she has a new baby. Mr. Bertram Johnson has a wife, but the poor thing has been in the insane asylum for six months and it seems she won't be getting out anytime soon, so he says he's rented his big house.''

There are more people here than there were in the farmhouse, Bonnie thought. She had longed for the privacy and quiet her mother had spoken of whenever she talked about her childhood in this house.

"Which room was Mama's?" Bonnie asked quietly.

"Why, you're in it," Winnie said, smiling. She reached out and smoothed Bonnie's hair back from her forehead. "She and her mother shared this room when she was a baby. She loved the view of the city. There was an airtight stove here then—we never should have taken it out. You'll be sleeping in your mother's old bed. What do you think of that?"

Bonnie blinked back tears. "I think it's wonderful," she whispered.

Before she went to bed, she began another letter to her best friend.

Dear Elena:

I'm glad to be in Cousin Audra's house, but I don't think I should have come. She seems to have fallen on hard times and has taken in boarders. Still, everyone is very kind to me except Clare, who is twelve and seems to resent me. We share a bedroom, so that makes everything difficult.

I'll write more later.

Bonnie was asleep before Clare came upstairs, and she slept all night long, but her sleep was troubled with dreams of the man in the train depot and Aunt Suze. When Clare woke her early, to tell her that breakfast was always served at seven, she was relieved to be rescued from her nightmares.

Clare was dressed already, and she didn't wait for Bonnie, but clattered downstairs without her. Bonnie dressed nervously, wishing she had awakened to find herself in the middle of next year, when everything wouldn't seem so strange.

Mrs. Younger had slept on the couch in her son's room and planned to leave after breakfast. She was pleased, she said, with everything about the house and she knew her son would be in good hands. Carson Younger said nothing, but came to the table and sat in silence.

Mrs. Marshall served pancakes, eggs, bacon, ham, applesauce, biscuits, and blackberry jam, along with coffee, tea, and buttermilk. The dining room was bright with sunlight, and even Clare seemed in a better mood.

Mr. Partridge and Mr. Nickerson ate quickly, in silence. But Mr. Johnson interrupted Audra's conversation with Mr. Younger several times to ask blunt questions of the blind man and his mother, and Bonnie thought he was ugly and rude.

Mr. Younger acted as if he had not heard any of the questions, but his mother, her narrow face flushed with annoyance, did her best to answer and then change the subject. It was obvious to Bonnie that neither of the Youngers wanted to discuss exactly how the young man had lost his sight. But that information was what Mr. Johnson wanted most.

Finally Mr. Younger got to his feet and stumbled away from the table. His mother hurried to catch up, and guided him out of the room.

Cousin Audra fixed Mr. Johnson with her cool gray gaze. "Mr. Younger is a hero," she said. "We must respect his desire for privacy."

Mr. Johnson's heavy face reddened. Bonnie could have cheered.

"Yes, yes," Mr. Partridge cried, waving a fork at Mr. Johnson. "We old fellows must honor the young men who have gallantly risked everything in the war."

"We all agree that you are right, dear Audra," Winnie said smoothly. "Does anyone else want another cup of coffee? Well, then, I'll help Mrs. Marshall clear the table and we can all be on our ways."

Bonnie suspected that Mr. Johnson wasn't finished with breakfast, but Winnie had made it impossible for him to linger at the table, since she whisked his plate away and smiled charmingly at him as she did so.

"Good-bye until this afternoon, Mr. Johnson," she said. She turned her back and carried the plate away.

"You never know about these fellows who claim to be wounded soldiers," Mr. Johnson huffed in an attempt to defend himself. "The city's full of them, begging on street corners for handouts. I say round them up and put them in jail until they prove they aren't Wobblies, here to make trouble for us at the shipyard."

"Mr. Younger is not a member of the International Workers of the World, nor is he a union member threatening to go out on strike against you," Audra said, with such reassurance that Mr. Johnson's color returned to normal.

"Can't be too careful," he said as he got to his feet. "Have to check these fellows out."

As Bonnie watched him strut out of the dining room, she heard Clare's faint giggle.

"Clare," Sally said warningly. "No one asked for your comment."

"And I didn't make it, either," Clare said. "Not yet." Her daring caused Sally to scowl, but Clare leaped up and ran out before her mother could scold her.

After breakfast, the dressmaker and her silent assistant came with boxes of dark blue uniforms and white blouses. Bonnie would have two uniforms by the first day of school, the woman promised, and two more by the end of September.

Sally left for the library, Mrs. Younger kissed her son good-bye and departed for the steamer, and Mrs. Marshall, wearing an immense, drooping black hat, went shopping. The day grew warmer.

Audra and Bonnie rode the streetcar downtown at two and returned at four, with shoes, stockings, a heavy dark blue winter coat, and a waterproof coat for the rainy days.

At the boarding house, they found Mr. Nickerson sitting on the porch, fanning himself with a newspaper and sipping lemonade. His face was lined with sorrow.

"You've been to your wife's grave, haven't you?" Cousin Audra said. She sat down next to him, stripped off her gloves, and reached for one of his hands. "Did I ever tell you that I often saw her at the matinee? And she was so helpful at the neighborhood house during the holidays. She had the sweetest laugh. Everyone said so."

Mr. Nickerson removed his eyeglasses, mopped his eyes with a clean handkerchief, and said, "Her laugh. Yes. It was so sweet."

Bonnie left them on the porch. Cousin Audra's kindness had brought tears to her eyes, too.

Clare was in the nursery, reading. When Bonnie came in, she demanded to see her clothes.

"They're exactly like mine," she said when Bonnie opened the boxes. Bonnie couldn't tell if she was pleased or unhappy.

"I asked Cousin Audra to pick things *you* thought were right," Bonnie said. It had been risky. She had known Clare might think she was copying her. But after all, their uniforms would be identical.

"It's a nicer coat than Marietta Nelson has," Clare said, satisfied.

Bonnie Rose felt a surge of hope. "Is that your red-haired friend I saw running off when I got here yesterday?" she asked.

Clare flushed, then laughed. "She's such a coward. She steals as much ice as I do, but Mr. Woffer would rather yell at me. He doesn't like us."

"I could tell," Bonnie said, and she laughed, too. " 'This house full of women!' " she quoted.

"Well, he can't say that anymore," Clare said. "The boarders are all men."

"I guess you aren't happy about taking in boarders," Bonnie said.

Clare shook her head. "Everybody at school will know when the new semester starts," she said. "Everybody will think we're poor. And I guess we are."

Bonnie shrugged. "Tell them your grandmother is only doing a favor for old friends of the family because she's so kind."

Clare looked at her with sudden interest. "Do you think the girls will believe it?"

"If you say it often enough," Bonnie said.

"Old friends of the family," Clare said, trying out the phrase. "Yes. That sounds nice. It sounds like the sort of thing Grandmother does all the time. Nobody would be surprised at that. After all, here you are, and you aren't even an old friend."

Clare returned to her book then, and Bonnie put away her new clothes in silence. She was a long way from having Clare as a friend.

I miss Elena, Bonnie thought as she turned a page. She's so easy to talk to. And she never hides sharp hooks in her words, the way Clare does.

* * *

Mrs. Marshall had complained loudly while preparing dinner that she didn't believe she could do the extra work for long. Her niece, Della, was willing to work every day, she said. Unless Della was hired, Mrs. Marshall didn't believe she could stay on, she said.

Bonnie had been sitting in the small back parlor next to the kitchen, reading one of Winnie's magazines, when she overheard Mrs. Marshall's complaints. She found Cousin Audra in the pantry between the dining room and kitchen, and offered to help in the kitchen, but Cousin Audra refused.

"Winnie and I can cut bread and fill water glasses," she said as she took glasses down from the shelves. "We'll have to do something about getting Mrs. Marshall a girl to help out, I suppose. But Della is so slow and clumsy. I swear that when she helps out here, we end up doing nearly everything for her. But still—"

"What would you pay her with?" Sally asked as she held open the swinging door for her mother. "The money from the boarders will barely pay the mortgages and food bills. Every cent I make will have to go for the bills we've got now."

"No one would have *dared* send your grandmother a bill," Audra said. Her pale face was flushed as she set the glasses on the sideboard.

Sally laughed. "Mama, I'm not sure there was such a thing as a bill in those days."

"There have always been bills," Winnie said disgustedly. She had spread a fresh linen cloth over the table, and was smoothing out wrinkles with her palms. "And women have always been left worrying about those bills."

"Well, what are we going to do?" Sally asked. "Mrs. Marshall wants help with the cooking, and not one of us can do much more than make toast."

"I can cook," Bonnie said. "Simple things, anyway. I cooked at the farm all the time. But I'm sure Mrs. Marshall could teach me anything else I need to know."

"It's out of the question," Cousin Audra said. "No child in this house will work in the kitchen."

The matter seemed to be settled. Dinner was late, and it was disappointing, compared to what Mrs. Marshall had served the night before. It was clear that she was punishing them.

At the last moment, Carson Younger asked Cousin Audra if a table could be set for him in one of the parlors. Bonnie, coming down the hall with roses Sally had cut for the table, stopped to listen.

"I'm not comfortable sitting at a table with strangers," he said quietly. "I'm sure you understand."

"Of course," Cousin Audra said. "I'll have the small table in the back parlor set for you. And I'll see to your plate myself, just as your mother taught me. Please don't be concerned about anything. But perhaps you might consider taking coffee with us afterward?"

"I don't think so," Mr. Younger said.

"I wish you would," Cousin Audra said. "It would make it so much easier for me. I don't know these men very well, and for some reason I feel that I know you better. You'll understand what they want to talk about, and I'm afraid that we women, well, we only bore them. I've been counting on you to get us through that awkward coffee time. Could you oblige me?"

Bonnie grinned. She knew he couldn't resist Cousin Audra's charming request.

"Of course, Mrs. Devereaux," Mr. Younger said. He sounded resigned. "But I don't know what I might say that would interest them."

"You're a war hero," Cousin Audra said. "They will respect anything you say on any subject."

It was true that first night, when Mr. Younger joined the others in the dining room for coffee. Bonnie was enchanted with him, his warm laughter, and his lean and handsome face. In his way, he could charm people as well as Cousin Audra. Only Mr. Johnson resisted, pouting silently at the table and excusing himself abruptly while Mr. Younger was telling Winnie about a concert he had attended in London before he had been sent to France.

Later, when she was alone in the nursery, she carefully tore a narrow strip of paper from her tablet and wrote on it, in small letters, "Please let me find a way to be of help." Then she slipped outside in the last moments of twilight, hurried across the lawn, and tied the strip deep inside the Ornament Tree where the leaves would hide it.

Mama, she thought, I'll do my best.

She pressed her fingertips to her lips to keep from crying. A slight wind shook the tree, disturbing the leaves. A ripe apple fell to the ground. Two faded strips of paper trembled with the leaves, and Bonnie wondered who had put them there. But she remembered what her mother had said. No one ever looked. No one ever told.

It was a clear, quiet evening, and Bonnie felt comfortable for the first time since she arrived.

But everything changed abruptly the next day.

4

*I*n the middle of breakfast the next morning, Mr. Johnson said, "I suppose you people have been reading in the papers that the Wobblies are threatening to take the unions out on strike."

"There is to be a general strike in the city, I hear," Sally said as she spread jam on her toast. "Well, you can't blame the poor souls. They don't know what will happen to them once the war ends and the layoffs begin."

"But they're communists," Mr. Johnson said.

"Nonsense," Sally said. Her voice was sharp, but amused. " 'Desperate' would describe them better. We must learn to be tolerant."

In the back parlor, Carson Younger tapped his spoon on his cup, a signal that he needed something. Clare leaped up and ran off. Bonnie would have gone, but Clare almost always beat her to the back parlor to serve the fascinating Mr. Younger.

Mrs. Marshall shoved open the swinging door to the dining room and carried in another pot of coffee. "There's fresh fruit, for them that wants it," she said.

She didn't smile or look at anyone, and set the pot down with a thud.

The people left at the table declined the offer of fruit, and Mrs. Marshall disappeared.

"We have to teach people that they're lucky to have any kind of job," Mr. Johnson said, and his voice began rising. "As soon as all the soldiers get back from the war, those men at the shipyard will find out that if they won't work for what we're offering, we can find plenty who will."

"Hoorah," Mr. Partridge said gloomily to his plate. It was obvious to Bonnie that the old gentleman despised Mr. Johnson.

Clare appeared in the door to the back parlor. "Mr. Younger wants to know who in hell is raising the racket, because it's giving him a headache."

The men at the table gasped at Clare's language. Cousin Audra's expression was unreadable, but Winnie laughed.

"Clare," Cousin Audra said flatly.

"Sorry," Clare said. "But that's what he said, and you've told me I should always repeat people accurately."

"Give me strength," Cousin Audra murmured to herself.

"All right, dear," Winnie told Clare. "Thank you for giving us the message. I'll explain to Mr. Younger that we've been discussing the possibility of a general strike."

"Well, that ought to make *him* happy," Mr. Johnson said bitterly.

Winnie barely made it through the door to the back parlor before Bonnie heard her laughter.

Bonnie stared at her plate to keep from laughing, too. She knew from Clare's carefully innocent expression that she had intended shocking everyone, and she had.

Oh, we could be friends! Bonnie thought. If she would only give me an inch.

Immediately after breakfast, Clare left for Marietta's house. She would stay there, she told Cousin Audra loudly while she looked sideways at Bonnie, until after the picnic lunch her friend had planned for a few girls in the neighborhood.

Bonnie found consolation in remembering that she was new to the family, and couldn't expect Clare to befriend her immediately. And Clare was also two years younger. That made a difference, too.

Probably, Bonnie thought, a picnic with those *infants* would be boring.

Sally and the men in the dining room left for work after breakfast. Cousin Audra and Winnie put on their hats and gloves and gathered up two stacks of books from the hall table shortly afterward.

"We're spending most of the day at the neighborhood house," Cousin Audra told Bonnie. "We're teaching arithmetic to the women today. But you'll find lots of things to do here. Take a peek in our little library next to the middle parlor. I'm sure we have books that will interest you. Or you could walk around our gardens. Paul—he's our handyman—has maintained it beautifully. He keeps white pigeons in the loft over the old stable, and they're pleasant company. Make yourself at home, child, and we'll see you at dinner."

"Thank you," Bonnie said blankly. She would be left alone in the house with Mrs. Marshall and Mr. Younger. But she couldn't feel at home yet. In fact, the idea of being alone here with strangers made her uncomfortable.

The women left in a flurry of interrupted comments and laughter, obviously glad to go to this neighborhood house, whatever it was. The house fell silent, except for

41

the clock in the hall and Mrs. Marshall's kitchen noises.

Mr. Younger tapped his spoon on his cup in the back parlor, and Bonnie ran to help. Perhaps he wanted to talk. She would be so pleased to have a conversation with anyone.

But he didn't want to talk. He wanted his tray taken away, and he didn't smile, either. He seemed angry.

"I'll take the tray, of course," Bonnie said nervously. "Is there anything else I can do for you?" she babbled, hating herself because her hands trembled and the dishes clattered on the tray. "Cousin Audra ordered extra copies of the morning paper. Would you like one?"

Mr. Younger cocked his head. "What would you suggest I do with it?"

She had done it again! When would she learn to avoid references to things that could only be accomplished with sight?

"I'm sorry," she said, close to tears. "That was stupid of me."

"Yes, it was," he said harshly.

"But," she began. "Well—"

"Bonnie, if you have nothing better to do, I would be grateful if you read a little of the morning paper to me," he said, his voice suddenly kind.

"That would be wonderful!" she cried. And then she wondered if she had said something stupid again. The only reason he needed anyone to read to him was because he was blind. That would hardly be called wonderful.

She fled to the kitchen with his tray before she could say anything even worse.

By the time she got the paper and returned to the back parlor, she had calmed herself enough to be able to sit down opposite Mr. Younger at his small table and ask him if he wanted her to start on the front page.

"If you please," he said. "Read me the headlines first. If something interests me, then I'd like to hear the whole article."

Bonnie dutifully read him headlines about the war in Europe, shipyard workers threatening to strike, crowds in New York streets complaining about the latest food regulations, and the first mail delivered by airplane.

Mr. Younger shook his head at each headline. His fine light brown hair fell over his forehead and he brushed it back impatiently. She saw that he had cut himself shaving, and a small patch of dried blood marred his strong chin. She wanted to brush it away but didn't dare.

Finally he said, "Put the paper down, Bonnie. Talk to me."

Her heart thudded uncomfortably.

"What do you want to talk about?" she asked.

"I don't want to talk about anything," he said. "I want *you* to talk."

She blinked miserably. "What shall I talk about?"

He laughed rudely. "Oh, for heaven's sake, Bonnie. You sound as if you're about to weep and make a horrible mess of yourself. I'll ask you here and now to spare me your tears. Tell me about the people in this house."

"But I don't know anything about them," she said. "I got here at the same time you did."

"Tell me what they look like," he said patiently.

"Oh!" She could do that. In fact, she could do it very well indeed. "Cousin Audra is very beautiful, even if she's old. Actually, everyone here except Clare is rather old."

He laughed again. "What is old to you, Bonnie?"

"Well," she began uncertainly.

"Am I old?" he asked.

She almost said yes, but actually he wasn't old. It was his blindness that made he seem that way. He walked so cautiously and slowly. Every gesture was so carefully calculated. But he certainly wasn't old.

"No, you're not old," she said. She studied him carefully, suspecting that what she said next would be important to him, for some reason she couldn't understand. "I think you're younger than Sally. Are you, umm, twenty-eight?" Her voice wavered uncertainly at the end of the sentence, and now she worried that she had offended him.

"Oh, Bonnie," he said, and his voice almost broke. He shook his head slowly. "That seems very old to you, doesn't it?"

She almost said yes. But instead, she said, "No. It's not old."

He leaned back. "What would you say if I told you that I am only seven years older than you? I'm twenty-one."

Bonnie thought that seven years was a long time. She caught her breath—and saw that he heard. His face flamed.

"I'm not a good judge of a person's age," Bonnie said quickly. She wanted to die. "Now I can see where I made my mistake. You have a little gray hair at your temples, just like the pastor at the church Mama and I went to before she died. I thought he was old until Mama explained."

He sat up straight again. "I was twenty the day after I landed in France. I was blinded by an exploding shell two weeks later. All I remember of France is rain and mud."

His terrible words hung in the air. Bonnie refused to allow herself to get up and run. Seconds dragged out to a minute, and she couldn't think of anything to say.

"I've shocked you, haven't I?" he said. "I like to shock people sometimes. You don't know what war is like, you people sitting back here, complaining because you can't get all the sugar you want, whining about how you suffer because you're expected to give up meat every Tuesday and your bread is black now instead of white.''

Bonnie licked her numb lips. Tears burned in her eyes. ''No, we don't know what it's like,'' she said. ''But if you want to tell me, I'll listen.''

''No, you *won't* listen, Bonnie,'' he said. His mouth twisted bitterly. ''My own mother won't listen. 'Don't think about it anymore,' she says. 'Don't talk about it and you'll forget about it.' ''

''But you're blind,'' Bonnie blurted. ''How can you forget?''

He smiled at her. ''Exactly, young lady. I'm blind, so how can I forget?''

Bonnie squirmed miserably in her chair. ''Do you want me to read anything from the front page?''

''No,'' he said. ''Look through the paper and see if there's something about books. Or plays. I'd like to hear about plays.''

Bonnie found the page that described Seattle's entertainment, and read a short article to him about a local production of *All's Well That Ends Well*.

''Do you like Shakespeare?'' he asked when she finished.

''Yes,'' she said.

''Then perhaps you'd read a play to me.''

She shook her head, then remembered he couldn't see her. ''No, I could never do that. I'd spoil it. But if you like books, I'll read one to you. Cousin Audra has a library here. And Sally works in the public library. We could get anything for you.''

''Can you indeed?'' he laughed softly, but she was certain he wasn't amused. ''Well, we'll talk about it later. I'm going out to the porch now and listen to the wind in the Ornament Tree. Perhaps I, too, shall tie a paper strip on it and make a wish.''

She fled before he got to his feet, telling him goodbye as she rushed through the door to the middle parlor. She pitied Mr. Younger and wanted to help him, but at the same time, she felt threatened by his mockery.

Let Clare wait on him after this, she thought furiously as she opened the door to the small library tucked in next to the middle parlor's wide bay window. Books filled cases that stretched from the floor to the high ceiling, and a rolling ladder stood to one side. To work off her pent-up energy, Bonnie climbed the ladder and chose a book from the top shelf. When she had made herself comfortable on the small leather sofa, she saw that she had taken down an old medical book, one devoted to the human spine and its deformities. She dropped the book beside her and burst out laughing. She knew Cousin Audra's long dead husband had been a doctor, but she had expected the library to represent the tastes of the women in the house.

''A house full of women,'' the iceman had said.

The men were spoiling that, and Bonnie wondered if Cousin Audra and Winnie thought so, too. Men were not easy to understand.

Clare returned in the middle of the afternoon, hot and disheveled, and thirsty for lemonade.

''Where's Mrs. Marshall?'' she demanded of Bonnie, who was reading *The Star Rover* on the side porch.

Bonnie looked up in surprise. ''Isn't she in the kitchen?''

''Would I be asking where she is if she were?'' Clare said. ''I looked in her room, too. I thought maybe she was taking a nap, but she's not.''

"Where's her room?" Bonnie asked, mystified. The house was large, and sprawled off into one-story wings and small additions toward the back of the long lot. Bonnie could barely find her way around the main part of the house.

Clare frowned. "For heaven's sake, Bonnie. Her room is next to the laundry, but that's used as a storeroom now. Haven't you looked around?"

"No one told me I could," Bonnie said shortly, and she returned to her book, seething. If she had taken it upon herself to explore all of the house, Clare probably would have accused her of snooping.

"Did she go shopping?" Clare demanded. "She's supposed to do that in the morning."

Bonnie put the book down. "I don't know if she did, but she was here to fix lunch. I don't know where she is now, but you could look in the icebox and see if she made lemonade."

Clare flounced around the corner to the back porch and Bonnie heard the door to the icebox open and slam shut. "No lemonade," Clare called out. She clattered down the back steps to the yard, and Bonnie heard nothing more from her.

Almost immediately the front doorbell rang. She waited, hoping that Mrs. Marshall was somewhere in the house and would answer it. The bell rang again, and Clare didn't come back, either because she was too far away to hear it or didn't want to.

Mr. Younger was upstairs, and Bonnie was sure the ringing disturbed him, so she got to her feet. Which way to go? Around the side porch to the front porch, or through the house? That would seem more formal. Bonnie hurried through the parlor to the hall, and then the front door. Through the stained glass, she saw the outline of a stocky man.

She opened the door. "Yes?" she asked cautiously.

"Well, now, who are you?" the man demanded, smiling.

Bonnie swallowed. "Are you here to see Mrs. Devereaux?" she asked.

His smile vanished and his heavy face fell into a sullen expression that seemed more natural to it. "No, I'm not here to see Mrs. Devereaux," he said sharply. "I'm here to join my wife."

Wife? Who could that be? Winnie was a spinster, and Cousin Audra had said that Sally's husband had run off—

Sally's husband?

Oh, why wasn't Cousin Audra home? Bonnie had no idea how to handle this. If he was Sally's long missing husband, should he be let inside? Any decision she made could be terribly wrong.

Mr. Younger glided downstairs, one hand on the rail, his cane pointed out before him. "Bonnie, do you need assistance?" he asked smoothly.

She turned to him gratefully. "There's someone here—" she began.

"I heard," Mr. Younger said. "Now, sir, will you introduce yourself so we know to whom we are speaking?"

The stout man on the porch stared rudely at Mr. Younger, lingering over his dark glasses and then his expensive summer suit.

"Who are you?" he demanded.

Mr. Younger smiled gently. "I believe I asked first, sir. Who are you?"

"I'm Jacob Harris," the man said. "My wife lives here. Is she home now?"

As he spoke, he stepped forward aggressively, and since Mr. Younger couldn't see him coming, the two men nearly collided. "Excuse me," Mr. Harris said sharply. "You're in my way."

Mr. Younger didn't budge, but he raised his cane and held it with both hands across his body to form a barrier. "Mrs. Harris is out, so you'll have to return later," he said evenly. "Bonnie, would you be kind enough to close the door when this man leaves?"

Bonnie shoved the door slowly, giving Mr. Younger a chance to step back. Mr. Harris was shut outside, the door in his face.

"I'll be back!" he shouted. He slammed his palm on the door for emphasis, and the stained glass panel trembled in its frame.

"I'm certain of it," Mr. Younger said, grinning mirthlessly. "Your sort always come back."

Bonnie and Mr. Younger listened while the man left the porch. His hard heels clicked on the walk.

Mr. Younger let out the breath he had been holding. "I believe things are about to become complicated," he said. "From what I overheard Mrs. Devereaux saying, I gather that this Harris fellow has been away seeking his fortune one place or another for most of Clare's life, and the ladies have been hoping against all hope that he died."

Bonnie stared. He had eavesdropped and learned that? No one had said as much to her, and she was family.

"Maybe he won't come back before Cousin Audra and Winnie return," Bonnie said. "They'll know what to do."

"I hope so," Mr. Younger said. "We're afflicted with this loud Johnson fellow from the shipyard. I'm not certain our jolly band could stand up under two men who learned their manners in the same school as the Kaiser. They blast everybody first and let God sort out the innocent from the guilty. Am I correct, Bonnie?"

"My aunt Suze is like that, too," Bonnie blurted.

"Ah!" Mr. Younger said. "At last I have some personal information from the maiden with the silky hair."

Bonnie's blush stung. She cleared her throat and said, "Clare's outside. Should I tell her that her father was here?"

"I wouldn't," Mr. Younger said. "You and I can safely claim ignorance and watch what unfolds at dinner tonight. I'll be sorry to be in the next room, perhaps missing some of the softer voices, but you can fill in the gaps later."

"You could sit at the table."

His humorless grin faded. "No, no. The present arrangement satisfies me. I'll feel free to comment, if necessary."

Clare ran up the steps, her arms filled with late summer flowers. "I'll fix the vase for the dinner table," she said. "Mrs. Marshall's back, Bonnie. Why didn't you come out to the garden and tell me?"

"I didn't know," Bonnie said.

Clare leveled a cold look at Bonnie, then at Mr. Younger. "You'd better come and help, Bonnie. Mrs. Marshall's brought that stupid Della with her, so we'll have to set the table all over if she does it. She puts all the spoons in a glass and sets it in the center. Can you believe it?"

"It's early yet," Bonnie said. "We have plenty of time to set the table."

Clare flounced through the door. "It takes ages to set a proper table for guests," she said. "It's not like slinging old plates and tin forks around for farm hands."

Bonnie, scarlet, watched Clare disappear into the dining room. That wretched girl!

"Before you lose your temper, think about this," Mr. Younger murmured. "Mr. Johnson, of the bellowing voice, will be here for dinner, which is enough to kill the appetite of a stray dog. And Clare's long-absent father is about to make his debut into our circle. Nothing you could wish on Clare will be half as bad as what is waiting for her."

He was right. Mr. Johnson was quarrelsome and rude, interrupting everyone at the dinner table in midsentence and scowling at Clare especially, because she dared to try talking to her mother during the meal. He helped himself without waiting to the best cuts of meat on the platter. When gentle Mr. Partridge said he felt sorry for the group of war widows he had seen gathered downtown holding up signs asking for pension money, Mr. Johnson denounced them and said they should apply to their families for help if they needed it.

Cousin Audra and Winnie stared frankly at him, and when Cousin Audra tried to change the subject, Mr. Johnson interrupted her.

He had launched into a harangue about the cowards who refused to go overseas to fight in the war when the doorbell rang. Mr. Harris! Bonnie had told Cousin Audra about his visit when she arrived home, but she didn't know if anyone else had heard about him yet. Sally and Clare seemed relieved at having Mr. Johnson's monologue interrupted. What would they think when they learned about Mr. Harris?

Cousin Audra went to the door and came back a moment later, her face blank but a little pale. "Sally, could you join me in the hall for a moment?" she asked.

Sally got up and left. Clare stared around, mystified.

Mr. Johnson glared out from under his eyebrows. "Who's that?" he demanded. "Who's interrupting dinner?"

"What new hell is this?" Mr. Younger caroled from his little parlor. Bonnie could hear the laughter in his voice and was caught between scandalized glee and cold fear at his daring. Mr. Nickerson hid a grin behind his napkin.

Mr. Johnson scowled toward the door that led to the small parlor. "I don't like having that man in there, listening to us," he told Winnie. "He should be out here, speaking his mind like a man."

Winnie leaned forward and smiled at Mr. Nickerson. "I've heard that your department store has been doing very well in spite of shortages brought on by the war," she said. "Haven't you had trouble finding people to work there?"

He smiled gratefully. "No, indeed. We pay more than the other stores. More than the unions require."

"The unions will ruin the country!" Mr. Johnson shouted. "Communists! If they strike the shipyard, we're ready for them. We'll have the Pinkerton detectives on them and smash in a few heads. That will teach them."

"Bravo!" Mr. Younger cried joyously from the parlor.

Mrs. Marshall pushed open the door. "Does anyone want more chicken? Potatoes?"

"Bring more of everything," Winnie told her. "We're all starved tonight. Isn't the chicken delicious? Mrs. Marshall is a wonderful—"

"I'll wager you don't pay *her* union wages," Mr. Johnson huffed.

Mrs. Marshall, carrying a platter of chicken, pushed open the swinging door and said, "They don't pay me nothing anymore," as she set the platter down. "Not for three months." She left the room immediately, her shoes squeaking on the carpet. The door swung shut. No one spoke for an eternity.

Winnie sighed. "May I serve anyone chicken?"

Mr. Younger's spoon rang against his glass in the

back parlor and Clare ran off to see what he wanted. Bonnie longed to go. She felt like a butterfly pinned to a wall. This was terrible! Cousin Audra should come back and take charge of the conversation before things got any worse.

Mr. Harris appeared in the doorway, well-groomed and freshly shaved. "Good evening, ladies, gentlemen," he said, smiling as he looked around. He tucked his thumbs neatly into his vest pockets and stuck out his chest. "Sorry I was late, but business held me up. Sally, will you set a place for me? Right here will do, at the head of the table."

Everyone stared. Mr. Harris was aware of their shock and he took full advantage of it. As Sally, white-lipped, put a plate and silverware in front of him, he looked around the room, smiling, drawing out the suspense.

At last he said, "I am Jacob Harris. I have just returned from Nicaragua, yes, indeed." He rubbed his hands together. "Opportunity lies to the south, gentlemen. Riches beyond belief, riches that spring from careful planning and cooperation with the right people."

"What do you mean, *cooperation*?" Mr. Johnson exclaimed, his face mottled. "Those people down there aren't white. You don't cooperate with savages, you tell them what to do!"

"Yes, indeed," Mr. Harris said, nodding briskly. He grabbed the fork Sally put down next to him and stabbed a large chicken leg. "We see eye to eye, sir."

"And I do, too!" Mr. Younger called out enthusiastically from the parlor. "Eye to eye."

"It's that blind fellow I saw earlier!" Mr. Harris cried, turning his chair to face the door to the parlor. "I recognize his voice!"

"Oh, be still my heart," Mr. Younger said. "I am known even among the yahoos. What can be next?"

"What the Sam Hill is he talking about?" Mr. Johnson demanded, looking around the table, his head lowered and his eyes bulging.

"Chicken, anyone?" Cousin Audra asked, smiling gently. "Mrs. Marshall cooks such lovely chicken."

Bonnie saw Clare in the doorway, staring at her father, with her fingers pressed against her mouth. Her face changed from white to pink. At last, she said, "*Father*? You're my father?"

Mr. Harris seemed to see her for the first time. "My word. Is that you, little pink pig-piggie? I haven't seen you since you were a baby. Look how you grew!"

Clare ran from the room, weeping noisily.

" 'What rough beast, its hour come round at last, slouches toward Bethlehem?' " Mr. Younger intoned morbidly from the parlor.

"Who *is* that fellow?" Mr. Harris demanded.

"Bonnie, run and ask Mrs. Marshall to serve dessert now," Cousin Audra said, smiling as if nothing was wrong. "I'm certain it will be delicious."

"Yum," Mr. Younger said from the parlor. "Delicious."

5

*L*ater, at Cousin Audra's suggestion, Bonnie carried a tray with two generous helpings of peach cobbler upstairs to the nursery.

Clare stood at the window, wiping her eyes on a sopping lace-edged handkerchief not much larger than a scrap.

Bonnie put the tray down on her desk. "Here," she said as she took a large handkerchief from a drawer. "No one can have a proper cry without a big handkerchief."

Clare hesitated a moment, and then reached behind with one hand for the handkerchief. Bonnie said, "Wipe your eyes and blow your nose. I've brought us our dessert and a message from your grandmother."

Clare looked over her shoulder suspiciously. "What did she say?"

Bonnie picked up one plate and a fork. "She said Mr. Harris won't stay long because she and your mother won't let him. You can talk to him if you want, but if you don't, then you can have your meals in the kitchen or in the parlor with Mr. Younger, if he's willing."

Clare whirled around. "Really? She said I could eat with Mr. Younger?"

"If he says so," Bonnie said. "He's awfully cranky, though. He says he won't have coffee in the dining room again, no matter how much Cousin Audra begs."

Clare sighed. "I guess I don't want to eat with him." She took her plate from the tray and sampled the cobbler. "Maybe I'll eat with Mrs. Marshall. I'm not going to sit in the dining room and be insulted every night by my own father."

Bonnie reflected a moment on the nickname Clare's father used for her. Pig-piggie? How terrible. But she had more news, and it might not suit Clare as much as being excused from the dinner table.

"You won't be sitting with Mrs. Marshall," she said, carefully keeping her gaze on her cobbler. "She quit."

"She did not!" Clare cried indignantly.

"She did," Bonnie said. "Right after she served dessert. She told Cousin Audra that she hadn't been paid and she was tired of cooking for so many people, especially since more people keep wandering in, and who knows where it will all end. And somebody named Fink had offered her a better position."

"Mrs. Savannah Fink hired her away from Grandmother?" Clare said.

"Mrs. Marshall must have already packed, because she left right away."

"What are they going to do?" Clare asked.

"Cousin Audra says they'll find another cook, but until then, she and Winnie and your mother will cook."

Clare burst out laughing. "Don't be silly. They can't cook." But then she sobered. "This might not be too bad. They really can't cook. The men will hate the food and leave, and nobody at school will ever find out they were here."

Bonnie considered scraping up the last delicious bits of cobbler with her fork, but scraping was unacceptable behavior, so she put her fork down reluctantly.

"Winnie and Cousin Audra are worried," she told Clare. "They can't lose the boarders because of the money they pay."

"Then my father will have to give my mother money," Clare said. "He never did, not one cent, not in all these years. Mama thought he was dead because he never even wrote to her. He'll have to make up for it now."

Bonnie doubted that Mr. Harris would prove to be of help. He reminded her unpleasantly of the traveling salesmen who showed up at farmhouses peddling useless odds and ends out of their suitcases. They could be very persuasive, but most of them were no better than thieves.

"Probably he'll be glad to help," Bonnie said, doing her best to sound certain.

Clare gnawed her thumbnail. "I suppose your father was perfect," she said, scowling.

"I don't remember him very well," Bonnie said. She knew Clare was embarrassed, and not only because of her father's behavior during dinner. Clare had revealed too much about his treatment of her mother and now she was sorry.

But Bonnie's mother had kept the memory of her father alive during their difficult years alone on the farm. He had been a good father and husband. She wanted to tell that to Clare now, but she had to be careful. If this was to be her home—and at the moment it didn't seem as if it was a very secure home—then she had to befriend Clare. Clare didn't make it easy.

"Is everybody in the front parlor?" Clare asked.

"Three of the men went for a walk," Bonnie began. "They've gone to the Harvest Home Hotel to drink whiskey in the bar," Clare said with disgust. "Grand-mother doesn't allow spirits in the house."

"Your father went with them," Bonnie continued. She stacked the plates on the tray and carried it to the door. "Your mother is reading a magazine to Mr. Younger on the side porch. Cousin Audra and Winnie are in that little cubbyhole under the stairs, calling people on the telephone."

"Looking for a cook," Clare said. "I hope they don't find one."

"Can't they even cook breakfast?" Bonnie asked.

Clare shook her head slowly, grinning. "No."

Bonnie shrugged and carried the tray away. Cousin Audra had written her after her mother died, telling her how important it was for every girl to be educated well enough to support herself and not rely on a husband to take care of her. Apparently the college-educated women in the house never stopped to think that they might also need to learn to cook for themselves.

Wouldn't Aunt Suze laugh at them if she knew? She had been right when she told Bonnie that she had managed quite well without schooling.

The kitchen table was heaped with dirty dishes. In the sink, pans soaked in greasy water. The room was hot, because Mrs. Marshall had used the wood stove as well as the gas range. Flies buzzed on the inside of the windows and crawled over the table and the cluttered wood drainboard beside the sink.

Bonnie opened the back door and all the windows to air out the room and let the flies escape. It was obvious to her that no one in the house connected cleaning the kitchen with the meal they had eaten an hour and a half earlier. Well, she could clean a kitchen.

She had finished when Winnie pushed open the swing-ing door and said, "My stars, child, but you gave me a start! I heard dishes clattering in here and thought for a moment that Mrs. Marshall had come to her senses and returned. And then, when I saw you, I thought I was dreaming. You didn't clean this kitchen, did you? You did! Why?''

"It needed it," Bonnie said as she twisted a dishtowel nearly dry, snapped it smartly, and hung it from the line strung across a corner of the room. "Have you found someone to cook?''

Winnie laughed weakly and pulled a chair out from the table. "No. No one we know can think of anyone looking for a position. We'll find one tomorrow, of course. We'll call one of the agencies, or try finding the right person at the neighborhood house. But most of the women who come there wouldn't be suitable. They don't understand basic hygiene yet. Sit here and rest, Bonnie. I'm going to fix us a nice pot of tea. I'm sure Audra would like that, too.''

"Let me fix it," Bonnie said. "But you'll have to show me how to use the gas range. I've never used one, and the fire is out in the wood stove.''

Winnie stared at the gas range. "I haven't the faintest idea how to turn it on. Won't they explode if you don't do it right?''

"I think so," Bonnie said. "I'll go ask Cousin Audra.''

"She won't know," Winnie said impatiently. "She's afraid of the thing and argued with Mrs. Marshall for months before she let her have one. Maybe Sally knows.''

Bonnie hurried out to the side porch, where Sally read to Mr. Younger in the last of the evening light.

"Do you know how to turn on the gas range?" Bonnie asked. "Winnie and I thought we might make tea.''

Mr. Younger cocked his head and grinned, waiting.

"Oh, dear," Sally said. "I saw Mrs. Marshall do it a dozen times, but it's very dangerous. I don't think you and Winnie should try."

"If Mrs. Marshall could learn how to use it, then I can," Bonnie said. "What did she do?"

"She turned a little handle and then held a match over one of the holes," Sally said. "It made a loud hiss and flames shot up."

"Oh, Lord save us," Mr. Younger muttered to himself.

"Would you like tea, Mr. Younger?" Bonnie asked him.

"I would prefer not being burned alive in a house fire, if I have that choice," he said.

"I take it that means you don't want tea ever again until the last trumpet sounds on Doomsday," Bonnie said, exasperated with his sarcasm. "You would help us if you showed a little patience." She left them in the twilight on the porch.

Infants! she thought. She would have died before letting them know how afraid she was of the gas range.

Winnie listened to the instructions and narrowed her eyes. "We can manage that," she said. "I'll turn the handle and you strike the match."

Bonnie would have preferred turning the handle because Winnie wouldn't see how her hand trembled. But she struck the match anyway, and was rewarded with a loud pop and a flame that rose two feet above the range.

"Great God!" Winnie cried, jumping back. "Get out of the way before you're burned!"

"What can we do?" Bonnie cried. Mrs. Marshall couldn't have cooked anything on a flame that high.

"I'll turn the handle back," Winnie said. The flame went out.

"Maybe you're only supposed to turn it part of the way," Bonnie mused.

"Of course," Winnie said. "Now we have the idea. Let's do it again."

Bonnie's heart thumped painfully as she took another match out of the tin box on the wall beside the wood stove. She struck it and held it over the hissing burner, and a smaller flame jumped up.

"I'll turn the handle back a bit more," Winnie said.

"Now it looks about right," Bonnie said. She filled the teakettle at the sink and set it over the flame.

Mr. Younger tapped on the door frame with his cane. "Is this the kitchen? I'm afraid to ask what's going on."

"We're making tea," Winnie said. "Where's Sally?"

"She went across the street to see someone named Bertha," he said. "Bertha has a gas stove and may know all the secrets to operating one without burning down the city."

"She has kitchen help who use the gas stove," Winnie said disgustedly. "Look at us! We are ridiculous. Half the women on this block want to vote, and not one of them can fix a meal for her family. Their cooks don't want to vote—Mrs. Marshall told me that—and they can manage everything in the households."

Mr. Younger grinned savagely and said, "My mother says that women are anxious to take their places beside men at the polls and in the world of commerce. Yet she seems quite proud when she tells people that her own mother had a personal maid and never dressed herself in her entire life."

Bonnie thought that if he had not been blind, he might have been shocked at the indignant expression on Winnie's face.

"Tea will be ready shortly, Mr. Younger," Winnie said. "Will you take it in the back parlor?"

"If you ladies will join me," he said. "I'll wait and pray that you survive this adventure in independence."

He blundered back the way he had come, bumping into the table in the pantry and then into the door that opened into the dining room. They should have helped him, Bonnie thought. But he was sharp-tongued, and he must have known how much he irritated people.

Winnie sighed. "I hope he keeps his opinions to himself," she said. "We can't afford to lose these boarders. But we should have everything settled by dinner tomorrow."

Bonnie, taking cups and saucers out of a cupboard, wondered dismally about the nearest problem, breakfast.

Later, when she climbed the stairs to the old nursery, Clare asked what she had been doing—and if her father had returned.

Bonnie flung herself down on her bed and jerked a pillow under her head. "They're all back," she said. "The men and Winnie are playing bridge in the front parlor. Cousin Audra and your mother are going through the kitchen, looking for recipes. They plan to cook breakfast themselves. I offered to help, but they won't let me."

"What's Mr. Younger doing?" Clare asked.

Bonnie sighed. "He's sitting in the dark in the back parlor, laughing at all of us."

Clare was silent for a moment. Finally, she said, "He's very handsome. Doesn't he make you think of Laurie in *Little Women*?"

"Laurie wasn't blind," Bonnie said. "And he was very polite. Mr. Younger is the rudest person I ever met."

"It's because he's suffering," Clare said. She got up and walked to one of the windows and looked out. "He is suffering," she repeated dramatically, and she drew herself up as tall as she could.

Oh, bosh! Bonnie thought. He'd be nasty even if he wasn't blind. He likes embarrassing people. Aloud, she said, "I don't think your grandmother would like to hear this conversation."

"So don't tell her about it, then," Clare snapped. "My goodness, Bonnie! Haven't you ever admired anyone?"

Bonnie thought of Mr. Younger's lean face and sensitive mouth. *Yes,* she thought. "No," she said. "Not in that way. I'm too young."

Clare laughed at her. "Marietta's mother married her father when she was fifteen."

Much later, Bonnie heard heavy footsteps climbing the stairs from the second floor. The footsteps passed their closed door and continued down the hall to the unused room next to the nursery. The door opened and shut, and someone coughed.

Mr. Harris. The women in the house were letting him stay for at least one night.

A moment later, lighter footsteps followed. Someone tapped on his door and opened it. Bonnie recognized Sally's voice, but she spoke too softly to be understood through the wall.

"I don't like this, Sally," Mr. Harris said clearly. "I don't like seeing boarders in this house."

Sally murmured something.

"Your father is dead, so I am the only man in the family. I say the boarders go. We can sell this place—"

Sally interrupted, and murmured again.

"We'll see about that," Mr. Harris said. "You don't understand the law as well as you think you do. Clare has an interest in this house because she'll inherit it someday, and I'm her father. I have to protect her against you and her grandmother.''

"The lawyer—" Sally said clearly.

"I have my own lawyer," Mr. Harris said smoothly. "You'll find out you can't have everything your own way."

The door opened and shut again, softly, and Sally's small feet hurried downstairs.

Clare stirred and sighed deeply. She had heard the conversation, and Bonnie was sorry for her.

Bonnie woke before six, dressed, and slipped quietly downstairs. Breakfast must be managed, and she knew best how to do it. But Cousin Audra and Winnie were there before her. Their hands and immaculate dresses were already streaked with black soot, the room was filled with smoke, and the back door stood open.

"What are you doing?" she asked them.

"Building a fire," Cousin Audra said. "Mrs. Marshall used both stoves for breakfast. But something seems to be wrong with the wood stove."

"Let me help," Bonnie said.

"No, no, certainly not," Cousin Audra said. "A kitchen is no place for a young girl. You can set the table for us, though. And bring in the newspapers from the porch."

"And fill the water glasses, please," Winnie said as she poked a small piece of kindling into the stove. A shower of ash poured out on the floor and drifted under the stove.

"The ashes have to be taken out," Bonnie said.

"We'll manage, dearie," Winnie said. "Now run along."

Bonnie let the kitchen door swing shut. All right, she

thought. Let them sort it out themselves. Mr. Younger had a point, even though he had presented it in the worst way. Perhaps it's time for the ladies to learn how to run a kitchen.

The table was set before the first boarder came down. Sally rushed through the dining room at the last minute, complaining of having overslept, and as she pushed open the swinging door to the pantry, a puff of black smoke escaped into the dining room. Bonnie smelled burned bacon.

What are they doing out there? she wondered.

Mr. Partridge puttered in, looking about like an anxious bird. "Am I first?" he asked. "Well, I'm afraid I'm quite hungry this morning." He took his place and sipped his water.

Mr. Nickerson followed him, rubbing his hands. "I can tell we're having more of that delicious bacon," he said. "Wonderful."

It won't be so wonderful, Bonnie thought. They've burned it.

Mr. Younger tapped his way into the room, sniffed the air, and smiled. "Bacon," he said. "Done to a crisp, if I'm not mistaken."

"Anything Mrs. Marshall prepares is delicious," Mr. Nickerson said.

Mr. Younger grinned wolfishly. "Indeed," he said. He tapped his way to the back parlor.

Bonnie had been afraid he would tell them that Mrs. Marshall was no longer presiding over the kitchen. She let out the breath she had been holding and moved forward with the water pitcher to refill Mr. Partridge's glass. "We're going to have another warm day," she said.

Clare, her braids water-slicked instead of done over, wandered in sleepily. "I smell burned bacon," she said.

At that moment, Sally opened the door to the pantry. A fresh white apron covered the soot on her dress. She carried a platter of pancakes, and she was followed by great clouds of billowing black smoke.

Everyone in the dining room could hear the peals of laughter coming from the kitchen, along with more smoke and the sharp, acrid odor of coffee that has boiled over on a stove.

"Pancakes?" Sally inquired brightly as she put the platter down on the table. The pancakes were scorched on the edges and the centers looked suspiciously soggy.

"I'll get the syrup and jam," Bonnie said quickly, and she hurried through the pantry to the kitchen.

Smoke billowed out of the woodstove and curled lazily along the ceiling before it escaped out the back door.

"You forgot to open the damper!" Bonnie cried. "What are you doing? Have you been trying to cook on it anyway?"

"It won't heat up," Cousin Audra said, bewildered. "The wood won't catch fire."

"It's because the fire isn't getting any air except through the open door," Bonnie explained as she turned the handle on the smoke stack. Immediately the sulking kindling burst into flame and no more smoke poured out into the room.

"The wood stove is going to take a long time to heat up enough to cook on it," she said. "Everybody's at the table except Mr. Harris. We'll have to use the gas range."

"But we're already using all three burners," Winnie explained.

Bonnie saw eggs scorching in one pan, coffee boiling over, and blackened bacon curled up in a frying pan. "This is hopeless," she said. "Have you sliced bread for toast? No? Don't you have anything to give them?

Is there any leftover applesauce from yesterday morning?"

Clare came in. "They want to know what's happening out here," she said. "Mr. Younger asked if someone should call the fire brigade."

Cousin Audra rolled her eyes toward heaven. "All right. We'll take this in stride. I'll go in and explain that they'll have to get breakfast downtown this morning."

That should be something to hear, Bonnie thought. She followed Cousin Audra and stood in the dining room door, listening.

"I'm so dreadfully sorry," Cousin Audra said to the men sitting at the table. She clasped her soft, small hands together in a charming gesture. "Mrs. Marshall left us unexpectedly last night, and we've had problems with the kitchen this morning. Would you please consider having your breakfast in the city today? I will reimburse you for the expense, of course."

Mr. Partridge got to his feet. "That won't be necessary, dear lady," he said heartily. "We'll get out of your way and let you women straighten out your household. Come along, gentlemen. Mr. Younger, can I assist you to the streetcar, or would you prefer walking?"

"I'll stay here, but thank you for the offer," Mr. Younger said. "I don't want to miss the excitement."

Mr. Partridge gave him a baffled look, but left with Mr. Nickerson. Mr. Johnson huffed and scowled, but followed after them.

"Thank heavens," Cousin Audra said. "Now. Let's put our heads together and solve our little problem."

Clare's father chose that moment to stroll into the dining room. "Where's all that smoke coming from?" he asked. "Where's breakfast?"

"I explained to you last night that I will not serve you

meals unless you pay for them," Cousin Audra said. "You didn't pay me last night."

"Well, I certainly wouldn't have paid for *this* one," Mr. Harris said. "You haven't let Sally loose in the kitchen, have you? She never could boil water."

"Excuse me," Cousin Audra said, and she turned her back on him. "Come along, Bonnie."

Bonnie looked over her shoulder at Mr. Harris. He watched Audra's departure through calculating eyes.

"Well," he said. The last Bonnie saw of him, he was striding through the hall, headed toward the front door. If he was disturbed by anything, it didn't show.

The women in the kitchen were laughing again.

They are like lambs going to the slaughter, Bonnie thought. She marched in and said firmly, "Now I'm going to show you how to use a wood stove."

6

The boarders endured three days of bad meals on the table, and smoke and laughter in the kitchen, before Winnie found a woman who had experience cooking for a large household and was willing to start immediately. Mrs. Terry refused to live in the house, however. She had a family, and wanted to return home every night. Her fifteen-year-old son James walked to the boarding house with her each morning at six and came for her again each night at nine.

"James doesn't go to school anymore," Clare told Bonnie one night as they were undressing. "He's looking for a way to make his fortune."

"Did you wait at the gate for him?" Bonnie asked. Cousin Audra had told Clare definitely that she should not hang about the gate waiting for the curly-haired boy.

"Grandmother didn't see me," Clare confessed. She stuffed her dress into a laundry bag, along with her underwear and stockings. The laundry woman was coming in the morning. "James is very nice, Bonnie. He works at the market on Saturdays, and you and I could walk over and see him."

"I don't think Cousin Audra would like that," Bonnie

said. "Mrs. Terry might not like it, either."

"All right, then I'll ask Marietta to go with me," Clare said. "Don't you ever have any fun, Bonnie?"

Bonnie, busy with the twelve buttons on her night-gown, thought that her idea of fun was different from Clare's, whose escapades were usually followed immediately by scoldings and banishment to the nursery.

But reluctantly, Bonnie had to admit to herself that she, also, thought James was nice. She had been sitting on the side porch one evening when James came for his mother. She introduced herself while he waited, and was pleased that he was interested enough to ask her where she had come from. She kept their conversation to herself, however. Clare would have been annoyed.

I'm not making much progress in befriending Clare, she added to her letter to Elena. *I'm not being of much help here, either.*

Bonnie and Clare started school the next day. The uniform was stiff and scratchy, but Bonnie loved it any-way. Cousin Audra had pinned a black armband to Bon-nie's jacket, explaining that the girls at the academy were taught to observe mourning of a family member for one year.

After breakfast, the girls pulled on their identical dark blue hats, shrugged into their matching jackets, and left for Miss Delaney's Academy for Young Ladies at ex-actly eight-thirty. This was the moment Bonnie had been waiting for. She loved school, and everything her mother had told her about the academy had pleased her.

"You'll stick up for me if the girls say anything about the boarders, won't you?" Clare asked her.

"How will they know if you don't tell them?" Bonnie asked.

"Because several of them live in our neighborhood,"

Clare said. "And everybody talks about everybody all the time."

"What about Marietta?" Bonnie asked. Sometimes she was almost jealous of Clare's friend.

"She won't say anything," Clare said. "I swore her to secrecy about the boarders and about my father, too. If she tells about me, then I'll tell everybody that her brother came home from college in the middle of last year because he got caught cheating on a test. She told everybody he had consumption."

"What?" Bonnie cried. "She said he had tuberculosis? But that's terrible."

"It's better than having everybody find out your brother's a cheat and a liar," Clare said as she skipped along the sidewalk.

Bonnie thought that Clare might be right, but she felt uncomfortable. What a choice to make!

The school was built of gray stone and rose three stories high, with intricate stained glass windows and gargoyles peering over the edge of the slate roof. A tall, elderly woman dressed in black waited inside the door and greeted each girl as she came in.

"Miss Delaney, this is Bonnie Shaster," Clare said.

Miss Delaney smiled. She was beautiful in a cold, impersonal way. "I remember your mother, Miss Shaster. I was sorry to hear that she passed away. But we are happy to have you with us."

Bonnie hoped she meant it. She looked back as they walked away, and saw her greeting another girl with the same smile.

"Isn't she wonderful?" Clare whispered. "She always wears black because when she was young, the man she was going to marry was lost at sea. That's so romantic."

Clare introduced her to several girls they met in the

71

halls, walked with Bonnie to her classroom, and then ran off with her friends. Bonnie entered slowly and looked around.

Four girls seated at desks looked back at her.

Bonnie's face burned. "Does it matter where I sit?" she asked.

The girls looked at each other and then back at her. "We sit in alphabetical order," a plump girl with bright blue eyes said. "Miss Carney will assign our places when she gets here."

Bonnie nodded.

"You can sit anywhere until she comes," a blond girl said. She smiled. "Who are you?"

Bonnie introduced herself, and learned that the blond girl was Charity McCall and the girl with remarkable eyes was Cristiana Lundgren. Before the other girls could tell her who they were, a short, thin woman with wiry hair escaping from a bun strode in. The girls stood up immediately, and Bonnie got to her feet, too.

"Good morning, ladies," the teacher said. She saw Bonnie and nodded. "Miss Shaster, I believe? I am Miss Carney. Welcome to the junior class. As soon as everyone assembles, we'll listen to Miss McCall read the school announcements, and then we'll begin our day. Ladies, please be seated."

Everyone sat as abruptly as they had stood.

Bonnie blinked. Her new life had begun. The last days had only been preparation for this moment.

Mama, she thought, here I am. Her fingers crept to the armband and adjusted it carefully. Mama, watch me make you proud.

Clare sulked on the walk home that afternoon. Everyone knew about the boarding house, she reported. At lunch in the refectory, several girls had asked her about it, and even though they pretended great interest, Clare knew they were laughing at her.

"This is all Grandmother's fault," she said. "And Winnie's. And Mama's, too. Why did they let us get to be so poor? I've never been so humiliated."

"I don't think you're poor," Bonnie said. "After all, you're still going to the Academy. You have everything you need and you live in a beautiful house. There are girls your age in Seattle who don't go to school because they have to work to help support their families."

"Oh, stop it!" Clare cried. "Please don't lecture me about all that child labor rubbish. Winnie goes on and on about it, and she and Grandmother pass out pamphlets about it—when they aren't passing out pamphlets on birth control."

"What?" Bonnie gasped. She stopped walking to stare at her young relative.

"Birth control," Clare repeated with obvious satisfaction at having shocked Bonnie. "Don't be stupid, Bonnie. Birth control is that business about women not having so many babies. There are things they can do, you know. Ask Grandmother. She'll give you a pamphlet, too. Maybe she'll stick one in your school bag, even though Miss Delaney told her she must not talk about it in the hearing of any of the girls from the Academy because some of their parents don't believe in it and go right on having babies every ten minutes."

Bonnie gawked at her in astonishment. Because she had grown up on a farm, she knew about reproduction. But birth control was illegal, a subject that had been only whispered about among the older girls at her old school. The younger girls believed what Bonnie had once believed—God gave ladies as many babies as He decided they should have, and of course, everyone preferred that the ladies were married when these events came about.

Bonnie had assumed that Clare, only twelve, believed the same, especially since she had grown up in the city, far away from the mating and birth events that took place in barnyards and fields.

"Close your mouth, Bonnie," Clare said. "You'll catch flies." She marched off, her chin held high.

Bonnie followed slowly. She had no idea what Cousin Audra would think of that conversation. Or Sally, either. Winnie might burst out laughing. Should she repeat it? No. But she thought that Clare was pushing her family to the limit.

Ahead of her, Clare caught up with Marietta and another girl, and the three of them laughed at something. Bonnie made no attempt to catch up.

There had to be a way to make friends with Clare, but she hadn't discovered it yet.

When she reached the boarding house, she found a thick letter from her friend, Elena, and took it upstairs to read and reread. Elena wrote that she had sent Bonnie many letters while she lived with Aunt Suze, and couldn't understand what had happened to them.

But Bonnie knew. Aunt Suze had kept them from her, and probably destroyed them. All through that hot, miserable summer, while she worried about her friend, Aunt Suze had known she was all right.

Elena reported that her father had found work in a motion picture studio, and Elena herself had seen the inside of the place, which was not as exciting as one might think.

I was sorry to move away from you, she wrote. *But I'm so glad to be here. We have our own orange tree growing in the back yard. What do you think of that?*

Bonnie could hardly wait to write and tell her.

*　　*　　*

After dinner, Mr. Younger tapped his spoon against his glass and Clare, complaining of being tired, asked Bonnie to see what he wanted.

"What are we having for dessert?" Mr. Younger asked Bonnie.

"Mrs. Terry baked apple pies. Shall I bring you a piece?"

"Bring one for yourself, too," he said. "I want to hear about school."

She took away his dinner plate and came back with their desserts and his coffee. "It's a wonderful school," she told him. "My mother graduated from it a long time ago."

"Not that long ago, Bonnie," he said. He touched his pie with one finger, used the finger as a guide, and cut into it with his fork. "But go ahead, tell me everything."

He finished his pie while she talked, and then held his coffee cup in both hands. His fingers were long and slender. Her mother would have called them musician's hands.

"Mrs. Devereaux told me this morning that you looked very smart in your uniform," he said. He cocked his head to one side. "But she said you have difficulty keeping your hair tamed. All the girls must have their hair tied behind their ears, she said, and you have little curls escaping everywhere."

Her hands flew to her hair. "I guess I do," she said.

"I wish I might have seen that," he said quietly.

They sat in silence for a long moment. Then he said, "Would you read a little of the evening paper to me?"

"Don't you want Clare to do it?" she asked.

"She's very young," he said. "She grows impatient with the things that interest me."

"The theater," she said. "Plays and books."

"Yes," he said. "Clare wants to read the latest fashion

news and the gossip about those fortunate people who are going to the concerts and plays.''

"You could go," Bonnie said hesitantly, "You could listen."

He turned his blind face toward her. "No, I can't go," he said. "Now, the paper? Would you mind?"

"I'd be glad to read to you," she said, and she ran out to get a paper from the hall table. Would she never learn not to hurt him with her tactlessness?

She interrupted a conversation in the front hall. Cousin Audra and Mr. Harris stood facing one another, and Cousin Audra's face bore an expression Bonnie had not seen before. Her gray eyes were cold as ice. She was holding several silver dollars in her hand, and as Bonnie watched, she dropped them into the pocket in her dress.

"This will be the end of it," Cousin Audra said to the man in a low voice. "Make no mistake about this. Today we listened to everything you had to say, and we rejected all of it. I expect you to be on the Portland boat in two weeks, as you have promised."

"I've paid you for my board, and more than it's worth, if you ask me," Mr. Harris said.

"No one asked you," Cousin Audra said. She turned and smiled at Bonnie.

"I only wanted a paper," Bonnie said, embarrassed. "I'm going to read to Mr. Younger."

Cousin Audra picked up a paper and handed it to Bonnie. "That's kind of you, dear."

"And another thing," Mr. Harris said. "I don't like the idea of my girl hanging around that blind fellow."

Cousin Audra walked away, guiding Bonnie with one hand on her elbow.

"I'm sorry," Bonnie said. "I didn't mean to interrupt."

"Providence must have sent you," Cousin Audra said. "The man is insufferable."

"Can I help?" Bonnie asked.

Cousin Audra smiled. "You can help by doing your best to forget him once he's out of our house."

Our house. Bonnie smiled back.

Night after night, she read to Mr. Younger for half an hour after dinner. He listened closely and sometimes asked her to repeat a sentence. Sometimes he smiled. Usually he seemed grave, even sad. He didn't want to hear about the war, although the men at the dinner table talked so loudly about it that he must have known all the news from Europe. The terrible war was drawing to a close.

But Mr. Younger was interested in several small items that had appeared regarding a new disease that had broken out in the East, first in Boston, and then spreading to other large cities. It was called "Spanish Flu."

"Have you heard about it before?" Bonnie asked him one night in late September.

"I read about something similar in a medical book once," he said. "Quite a few years ago, there was a great epidemic that killed many people in Europe."

"The Black Plague," Bonnie said.

"No, something different. The description of it sounded much like what we've been hearing about this new disease. It began like the ordinary flu we've all had. But very quickly it became deadly. And now it's returned. Or else something very like it has come. We shall see."

"Does it worry you?" Bonnie asked.

He cocked his head. "We don't know anything about these epidemics. If we cared as much about saving lives as we do about destroying them, perhaps we could find a cure."

"How do you know so much about these things?" Bonnie asked.

He grinned his terrible, savage grin. "Why, Bonnie, before I sailed off to the war, I had hoped to become a physician, like my father and my grandfather."

"I'm sorry," Bonnie whispered.

"What are you wearing?" he asked suddenly.

She looked down at her dress. "A pink cotton wash dress, one that Cousin Audra's dressmaker made for me."

"What is a wash dress?" he asked.

"It can be washed with the other simple laundry," she said. "It doesn't have to be dry-cleaned or done by hand."

"Ah." He leaned back in his chair. "Does pink become you, Bonnie?"

She blushed. "I don't know."

"I think you do. Tell me the truth. Does it become you?"

"Yes!" she said.

He laughed. "Tell me another truth. Have you tied a paper strip to the Ornament Tree since you moved here?"

"Yes," she said. She fidgeted uncomfortably, hoping he wouldn't ask more questions about it.

"Did it bring results?"

"Not yet."

"Keep me informed," he said, laughing again. "I can't wait to find out if a tree can grant what God can't. Or won't."

He was still laughing when she folded up the paper and carried it away.

I don't understand Mr. Younger, she wrote to Elena.

Sometimes he seems to hate everyone. Perhaps I would, too, if I had been blinded. But I wouldn't sit in my room all alone every day! I'd do something. I don't know what, but I'd do it.

7

⊰⊱✿⊰⊱

Autumn arrived early with rains so heavy that they
flooded basements in the houses at the foot of the hill.
Bonnie and Clare plodded back and forth to school under
a large black umbrella. They wore black rubber galoshes
to protect their shoes, but their dark blue stockings were
often splattered with mud.

Lightning split an old maple tree beside the school
during lunch one day. Several windows in the refectory
broke when the tree fell, frightening the youngest girls
into screaming. Mothers and nannies were summoned by
notes carried by the maids from the boarding annex,
since everyone knew that using a telephone during a
storm was dangerous. By one o'clock, all the day school
girls in the first three grades had been taken home. The
little boarders who had nowhere to go had been put to
bed in their dormitories with bread and milk and new
prayer cards for their instruction and entertainment.

"Let this be an opportunity for us to demonstrate our
courage and self-control," Miss Carney told the girls in
her class. Her face had been cut by flying glass, but the
girls sitting closest to her during the excitement reported
that she had held a napkin to her face without comment

and led everyone who had been sitting at her table to safety in the great hall.

This is where Mama and Cousin Audra learned to be so calm and strong, Bonnie Rose thought. I'll be that way, too.

That evening, Mr. Younger questioned her about school, the way he always did, and she told him about the tree and Miss Carney's bravery.

"You sound like somebody's governess and not our own Bonnie," he said.

She had been practicing speaking in a calm and composed voice, so his criticism stung her. For an instant, she was tempted to ask him who he thought he was, to make fun of her efforts to sound like an adult instead of a silly child. She hadn't been sent home with Nanny to weep in her mother's lap over a broken window!

But Miss Carney wouldn't approve of her losing her temper, either, so she said, "I was trying to tell you my news without editorializing."

He burst out laughing. "All right, young lady. Point taken. Now read the paper to me."

"Do you want to hear about the shows, or shall I find something about Spanish Flu?" She rustled the papers briskly, to let him know she was no one to fool with.

He sighed. "Is there more about it?"

"There's half a page," she said. "Many people are dying in the East. We're lucky we're so far away."

"Trains come here every day from the other side of the country," he said. "People carrying the disease might be in Seattle already."

For the first time she was frightened by what she read to him. He must have sensed her alarm, because he interrupted her halfway through the article and asked her to turn to the theater page.

Winnie brought tea in, along with slices of Mrs.

Terry's chocolate upside-down cake. Mr. Partridge, buttoned up in a heavy coat and on his way to the hotel for his after-dinner drink with the other men, stopped in to tell Mr. Younger that his brother-in-law's cargo ship had docked that afternoon, and he had brought a small crate of Japanese oranges to the house.

"I remember that you mentioned you had tasted one once and liked it," Mr. Partridge said. "May I offer a few to you and Miss Shaster?"

Mr. Younger showed more enthusiasm about the fruit than anything else, so Mr. Partridge trotted away and came back carrying a small basket filled with small, soft oranges.

"I hate to sound unkind," Mr. Partridge said. "But I'd be very grateful if you didn't let Johnson or Harris know about the oranges. Scoundrels, both of them. No, I don't wish to share with them."

"We are sworn to secrecy," Mr. Younger said. "Bonnie will dispose of the evidence the moment we finish."

"Good man," said Mr. Partridge. "You understand the situation completely."

Mr. Younger laughed briefly. "I can't help it, since both of them shout every word that pops out of their mouths. Do you think Johnson will go in with Harris on his South American scheme?"

"I certainly hope so," Mr. Partridge said. "The man is bound to lose every cent he invests, and I can't think of anyone I would rather see it happen to. They are both bad husbands. Disgraceful, what's happened to their wives. Nickerson and I are keeping our fingers crossed that they'll get what they deserve out of their scheme."

He went off, smiling to himself, and Bonnie laughed. "I don't know anything about the scheme you two were talking about, but neither of you seems to like Mr. Johnson or Clare's father."

"We look forward to their leaving the house," Mr. Younger said. "The sooner, the better."

"But Cousin Audra needs to have boarders here," Bonnie said.

"Surely she could find more compatible men," Mr. Younger said as he peeled the loose skin from one of the oranges. "You'd better eat one of these oranges before I gobble all of them."

Bonnie took one out of the basket, but her mind was on their conversation. "Cousin Audra says that it's hard to find even three people who can get along all the time, and we must be tolerant of everyone's shortcomings. Miss Carney says that we have a duty to be understanding."

Mr. Younger cocked his head and grinned. "I hear both of them speaking in your voice. But where is the Bonnie who defended Clare against the iceman and denounced me for being unsympathetic during the kitchen crisis?"

"I don't know what you mean," she said.

"I would hate to see you lose—" He stopped speaking and looked as if he was straining to hear something. "Wasn't Clare told she is not to hang around the gate with Mrs. Terry's son?"

"Is she out there again?" Bonnie said. She jumped up and tried to see out the window into the dark, but the light in the room reflected on the glass and all she saw was herself. But she heard what Mr. Younger had heard. Clare was out there, laughing with James Terry in the dark.

"I'd better go out and get her," she told Mr. Younger. "If Cousin Audra catches her, she'll spend the weekend in the nursery again." She opened the French door leading to the porch.

The moment she stepped outside, the voices at the side

gate stopped. "Clare, you can't stay out here," she said into the dark.

Neither of the culprits answered, so Bonnie walked briskly to the gate. James backed up a step when he saw her.

"Hello, James," she said.

He laughed softly. "We saw you through the window, talking to your friend," he said.

She wondered, with annoyance, if James had any idea how good-looking he was. Clare certainly did. Probably it would be best to ignore him.

"Clare, your mother and grandmother would both have a fit if they knew you were out here," she said.

"Then let them," Clare said, and to prove how independent she was, she boosted herself up and sat on the fence.

"It's cold out here and you aren't wearing a coat," Bonnie said. "Come inside. Or else."

"This is none of your business, Bonnie," Clare said. But she jumped down and flounced through the French door. Bonnie saw her pass Mr. Younger without speaking. And she saw Mr. Younger laugh.

"Don't go in yet," James said. He touched her arm.

She turned to look up at his face, barely visible in the dim light from the street lamps. "It's nearly nine," she said. "Your mother will be coming out in a moment."

He ignored her comment and smiled. "We hardly know each other, Bonnie," he said. "We'll have to do something about that."

"You hardly know Clare, either," she said crisply. Heavens, but he was handsome! No wonder Clare sneaked out to the gate nearly every night.

"She's only a baby," he said.

"Then don't encourage her."

"I'm encouraging you," he said. "I'll come earlier

tomorrow, and we can go for a walk around the neighborhood."

"Certainly not," Bonnie said, but her heart thumped. "Good night, James." She walked away before she could change her mind, and she shut the French door firmly behind her.

"So he wants to take you for a walk," Mr. Younger said.

"I'm not surprised that you eavesdropped," Bonnie said crossly as she dropped the orange peel in the basket. "There's nothing going on in this house that you don't know about—and make mean comments about."

"Here's Bonnie back again," he said, and he laughed. "It didn't take long for all that stylish elegance to wear thin."

Bonnie shoved most of the small orange in her mouth. "You're quite impossible, you know," she said.

"Didn't any of the ladies in your life tell you not to talk with your mouth full?" he said.

Dear Elena:

The cook's son is very good looking, and Clare is crazy about him. Her mother wouldn't approve, and not just because Clare is too young. James doesn't go to school, and this family puts great value on education. I wish I could stop thinking about him.

The Spanish Flu invaded Seattle on October first, and within days hundreds of people were infected with it. By October fifth, all public gatherings were forbidden. The theaters, churches, and schools closed. The hospitals were so crowded that people were dying on cots in the halls.

On October tenth, Cousin Audra told Bonnie that her classmate, Charity McCall, had died of the flu, nine hours after her baby brother died. On the following day, Charity's mother died. All three were buried together, without a funeral because of the ban on public gatherings.

On October twelfth, Clare's father announced that he was leaving Seattle on the Portland boat, and from there he would set sail for South America.

"Business waits for me," he said at the breakfast table. "I can't linger here any longer, no matter how pleasant the company has been."

Sally leveled a cold look at him. Clare pushed a bit of sausage around on her plate. Cousin Audra passed toast to Mr. Nickerson. Mr. Partridge suddenly coughed into his napkin, stood up, and left the table.

"I suppose that old fellow is coming down with the flu," Mr. Harris said. "Well, I've never had a sick day in my life. It's a waste of time, and time is money."

"Oh god," Mr. Younger groaned from the back parlor. "It's too early for philosophy, sir. Spare us."

Mr. Harris ignored him. He smiled at his former wife. "You'll be hearing from me soon," he said. He scowled at Cousin Audra. "I wasn't at all impressed with that lawyer of yours, Audra. No, I wasn't. I'll pursue the matter as soon as I return."

Cousin Audra raised her eyebrows but didn't speak to him. Instead, she said. "Winnie, would you like another piece of toast?"

Mr. Johnson watched Mr. Harris coldly. "I hope *I'll* be hearing from you soon, too," he said.

"Oh, by telegraph the minute I arrive in Portland," Mr. Harris said. "I'm sure the provisions for the voyage are already waiting at the dock, ready to be taken aboard."

"Hmm," Mr. Johnson said. He speared the last sausage on the platter.

Bonnie and Clare exchanged quick looks. It would be such a relief to have the man gone.

"Bonnie, would you see if Mr. Partridge needs anything?" Cousin Audra said.

Bonnie excused herself, but she didn't need to go to the second floor to offer Mr. Partridge help. He was standing at the far end of the hall, and he was laughing, not coughing.

"Are you all right?" she asked him.

"Never better," he said. He mopped his face with his handkerchief. "I suppose you already know that the women in this house are saints. If Mrs. Devereaux and her daughter had thrown Mr. Harris down the stairs, I would have cheered."

"I'd have helped," Bonnie said.

The illness took hold in Seattle. Each day the number of deaths was printed in the newspapers, and each day the number rose. Anyone going out on the street for any purpose was required to wear a mask.

The neighborhood house where Cousin Audra and Winnie taught skills to poor women so that they might find jobs had been closed the first week. They worried about the people they had been helping, but there was nothing they could do but wait. Sally's library remained closed.

Mr. Johnson told them that half of the workers at the shipyard were sick.

"But that's just fine," he said. "We don't have to pay them. The war is nearly over, and before much longer, we'll be getting rid of them anyway."

"Then the men who are left will go out on strike," Mr. Nickerson said.

"We'll teach them a thing or two," Mr. Johnson said. "Don't worry. We're ready for anything." He lowered his head and moved his bloodshot gaze from one end of the table to the other. "Don't feel sorry for those men. They'll get what they deserve."

His disposition, never pleasant, had grown much worse since Mr. Harris had left for Portland and then disappeared with a large amount of Mr. Johnson's money. Sally had not heard from Mr. Harris, either. But then, she had known better than to expect a message.

On October 21, the evening newspaper reported that thirty people had died that day alone from the flu.

In early November, the war in Europe ended, and the city went wild. The ban on public gatherings was lifted—but the people would have ignored it anyway. Men and women threw away their masks and surged into the streets to cheer and wave flags. The last of the soldiers would come home now. The horrors of the bloodiest war in history were over.

But the Spanish flu remained, although it had subsided.

School resumed the Monday after Thanksgiving, and the girls went back to discover that several classmates were still too ill to leave their beds.

The disease seemed to strike adults harder than children. Several sober-faced girls wore black armbands. Morning prayers lasted longer than before, and Bonnie, whose mother had been dead less than a year, often wept when small voices asked for prayers for a parent in heaven.

Christmas in the boarding house was a grand event in everyone's opinion. Mrs. Terry found both a turkey and a ham for Christmas dinner, and delighted Mr. Nickerson by starting the meal with the same kind of fruit soup his wife had always served.

"Merry Christmas," Clare told Bonnie that night after they had climbed into their beds. "This turned out to be a nice year after all. Especially since my father wasn't here to spoil the holidays."

Bonnie grinned in the dark. But she forced herself to sound very serious when she said, "We can hope that he had a fine holiday wherever he is, though."

Clare was silent for a moment, and then said, "Don't be so pious, Bonnie. Actually, I hope nobody gave him a gift and he went hungry."

Bonnie knew better than to laugh aloud. Clare often said terrible things about her father, but if Bonnie showed any sign of sympathy or agreement, Clare's temper flashed. She was proud and, Bonnie thought, still not a real friend. Not like Elena.

Dear Elena:

Thank you for the beautiful card. I can't imagine what it must be like to celebrate Christmas in a place that has palm trees instead of fir trees. We had a wonderful holiday, but I did feel sorry for Mr. Younger because he is so far away from his family. Do you have Spanish Flu in Los Angeles? I tied a note to the Ornament Tree, asking that this family be spared.

On the first Sunday in January, in the middle of the morning, Bonnie found Mrs. Terry sitting at the kitchen table, resting her head on her arms.

"Tired?" Bonnie asked.

The woman raised a flushed face beaded with perspiration. "I'm afraid I'm ill."

"I'll get Cousin Audra," Bonnie said quickly, and she ran from the room.

Spanish Flu had flared up again in the city. Sally's library had closed once more because most of the librarians were ill. The neighborhood house had opened after Christmas, but only a few of the women had bothered to come back.

Cousin Audra had been lingering over coffee in the dining room with Winnie and Mr. Partridge. Bonnie bent and whispered in her ear, in order to avoid alarming the others. Cousin Audra excused herself and hurried through the pantry into the kitchen.

Mrs. Terry was coughing and vomiting helplessly into a towel. The vomit was tinged with blood. When she raised her head, Bonnie saw that the skin around her mouth and nose looked blue. She trembled violently.

"Do you know where she lives?" Cousin Audra asked Bonnie. "She doesn't have a telephone, so I need you to run and get someone from her family. It's Sunday, so her husband should be there."

Bonnie grabbed her coat from the cupboard in the front hall and took off running. The Terry house was nearly a mile away on the streetcar line, in a shabby neighborhood behind the bus depot. Winnie had pointed it out to her once. On another day, the streetcar would have taken her there quickly, but the cars didn't run often on Sundays. Bonnie had a stitch in her side by the time she arrived.

She had to tell Mr. Terry twice that his wife was ill. He seemed very shaken and kept saying, "It won't be the flu, it won't be the flu." He told her he knew someone who might give him a ride in an auto and take his wife home in it, so Bonnie left.

The steep hill loomed ahead of her, and rain began falling. She burst into tears and started the long walk home. She was still several blocks from the boarding house when an auto went by, with Mr. Terry sitting stiffly in the passenger seat. He didn't see her. He stared straight ahead.

She found the auto parked in front of the house when she got there. Mr. Terry and his friend were in the front parlor, still bundled up in their heavy coats, pacing and whispering to each other. Mrs. Terry lay on the sofa, unconscious. Her breath rattled and whistled in her chest. Winnie murmured to Mr. Nickerson in the parlor doorway. Both watched Mrs. Terry intently.

Cousin Audra spoke on the telephone, her voice urgent. "But you must make room for her," Bonnie heard her say. "We have an auto here. We can bring her immediately."

Clare, pale and wrapped in one of her mother's shawls, sat on the bottom step hugging her knees. "Do you think she's going to die?" Bonnie heard her ask Winnie.

Winnie tightened her lips. "No, no, of course not. She'll be fine once she's in the hospital."

But Bonnie saw Mr. Nickerson shake his head sharply.

Mrs. Terry died an hour after reaching the hospital. Cousin Audra said that the doctor had told them the flu took people that way sometimes. Another doctor, a friend of his, had made a housecall on a man and was found dead two hours later in the room with his unconscious patient.

It was time for dinner when Cousin Audra returned from the hospital. Winnie and Sally had heated soup and toasted bread for the boarders. Only Mr. Johnson was hungry, but he rejected the soup and went to the hotel for dinner.

Mr. Younger sat at the table with them that evening. When they had all eaten what they could, he said quietly,

"Someone should see how the Terry family is getting along this evening. I thought Mr. Partridge, Mr. Nickerson, and I could look in on them."

"Certainly," Mr. Partridge said. "We can call a taxicab."

"I'll go, too," Cousin Audra said.

"Some of her things are still in the kitchen," Bonnie said. "Should I pack them so you can take them with you?"

"We'll do that in a few days," Cousin Audra said gently. "Not tonight."

The four of them left quietly a few minutes later. Clare watched the taxicab drive away and said, "I wonder how James feels tonight."

"He doesn't understand what's happened yet," Bonnie said. "I remember what it was like."

"I'm sorry!" Clare exclaimed. "I didn't mean to remind you."

"It doesn't matter. Let's go out to the kitchen, and I'll show you how to soak oatmeal for our breakfast tomorrow."

"I won't do any such thing," Clare said. "Why would I want to learn something like that?"

"We don't have a cook again," Bonnie said.

8

※~❀~❀

No matter how persuasive Bonnie tried to be, Cousin Audra would not allow her to cook in the boarding house.

"You do enough when you help me with the table settings and the serving," Cousin Audra told her as she added wood to a smouldering fire in the stove. "You have your schoolwork, just as Sally has the library. Winnie and I can manage the meals, and we'll find another housekeeper soon enough. I'm certain the boarders will understand."

She was mistaken. The men hated the meals, but only Mr. Johnson was rude enough to let Cousin Audra know. The others, including Mr. Younger, tactfully tasted everything that was put before them, declared themselves satisfied, and left for the hotel dining room.

Only Bonnie suspected that they did more than drink at the hotel.

"Tell me the truth," she said to Mr. Younger one evening after she finished reading the paper to him. "You eat dinner at the hotel, don't you?"

"Whatever gave you an idea like that?" he asked.

"You have a spot of gravy on your lapel, and we didn't have gravy tonight."

"We never have gravy," he said. "We have something Mrs. Devereaux *calls* gravy. If she were not so charming, I would suspect that she is trying to poison us."

"She's doing her best to be a good cook," Bonnie said.

"Nonsense," he said. "She and her fellow-conspirators wouldn't find so much to laugh at in the kitchen if they were doing their best to be good cooks. And surely by now they could have mastered that wood stove. The whole house reeks of smoke."

"Some of it comes from the coal furnace," Bonnie said. "They've been taking care of it themselves. Clare says they always had a handyman who managed the furnace after the weather turned cold, but he found a job in a lumber mill."

"And they can't afford to hire a new one," Mr. Younger said. "They don't charge us enough. Mr. Partridge has suggested that the four of us volunteer to pay more. It's the fair thing to do."

"Mr. Johnson agreed to that?" Bonnie asked, laughing.

"Well, no. But we might be able to shame him into it."

"Not him," Bonnie said. "The only one you'll shame is Cousin Audra. She'll think you're offering her charity."

Mr. Younger sighed impatiently. "She's as bad as my mother. They volunteer to help women they think are less fortunate than themselves, and it never occurs to them that they don't know enough, either, to be truly independent. All this fuss about votes for women. What nonsense. Men have already proven that elections are always won by the biggest crooks and liars. Do women think that they can resist being manipulated by clever words?''

Bonnie scowled at him. ''We should at least have the chance to vote.''

''*We?* It's *we* now, is it?'' He laughed. ''Is that what you're being taught at that fancy school of yours?''

''No, it isn't,'' Bonnie said. ''Miss Delaney doesn't allow conversations about votes for women or—'' She stopped before she blurted out the words ''birth control.'' Her face turned red and her tongue seemed to stick to the roof of her mouth.

Mr. Younger burst out laughing again. ''Oh, Bonnie, what would I do without you? My life would be endlessly boring.''

She jumped up. ''I have homework to do tonight,'' she said. ''Please excuse me.''

''Oh, of course, of course,'' he said. ''I would excuse you anything.'' He reached over and turned off the lamp that sat on the table near him. The room was dark.

''I wish you wouldn't do that before I get to the door!'' Bonnie Rose cried as she stumbled over the edge of the carpet.

''Even with the lamp turned on, you don't see what you should see,'' he said.

''What does that mean?'' she demanded from the doorway.

He sighed in the dark. ''Ask me again in a few years.''

She marched out into the hallway, angry again. He often left her disturbed and defensive, and she knew that he was aware of it and enjoyed it.

''Drat,'' she whispered.

''He got to you again, didn't he?'' Clare asked. She had been carrying a mug of hot milk upstairs, and she stopped to grin over the banister at Bonnie.

Bonnie hurried to catch up with her on the stairs. "I'd be glad to let you read to him," she said.

"Not I," Clare said. "I had enough of him. I still think he's the most romantic man I ever saw, but he makes fun of everybody. Half the time I'm not sure what he's laughing at, and that makes it even worse."

"I know," Bonnie said. "I know."

But she went back the next night, after he and the other men had returned from the hotel, to read to him again. The paper was full of news about the threatened general strike in Seattle, and the boarders had taken sides on the issue.

Who cares? Bonnie thought to herself more than once.

On the last Saturday of January, Cousin Audra brought someone home from the neighborhood house. The girl was no older than Bonnie, but she had been working as a cook for a year, and Cousin Audra had hired her to cook at the boarding house. The women in the family would do the housework themselves.

Bonnie was astonished when Melba Foss was introduced to her. Why would Cousin Audra allow that girl to work in the kitchen when she refused to let Bonnie do anything more than carry food to the table?

The girl was shorter than Bonnie, but she was already fully developed and slightly overweight. Her blond hair needed washing, but it was arranged in complicated puffs, curls, and stringy bangs. Her neck was very dirty. She acknowledged Bonnie's "How do you do?" with nothing more than a crooked smirk that displayed beautiful teeth.

"Where's my room?" she asked Cousin Audra. "You said I could sleep here."

"Come with me," Cousin Audra said, and the two of

them disappeared in the direction of the empty bedroom beyond the old laundry.

Clare, who had missed the introduction, arrived in the hall in time to see Melba strutting away behind her grandmother.

"Who is that?" she asked disdainfully.

"The new cook," Bonnie said.

"Is she old enough?" Clare was as amazed as Bonnie.

"Winnie says dozens of girls her age work as cooks and maids in Seattle."

"Well, I don't care, as long as somebody around here can cook something we can eat. I'm sick of meat that's burned black on the outside and bloody on the inside, and potatoes that are as hard as rocks, and runny pudding for dessert."

"You may not get anything better now," Bonnie said. "If Melba can cook, why didn't she stay at her last job?"

The next morning, Melba produced oatmeal without lumps, scrambled eggs, well-cooked sausage, and a large plate of nicely browned toast. It wasn't an elaborate meal, but it tasted better than anything the women in the house could make, and the boarders were pleased.

Bonnie was more pleased by seeing that Melba had washed her neck and pulled her hair back in a single long braid tied with a plain black ribbon that looked like silk. Cousin Audra must have made some tactful suggestions the night before. And provided the ribbon, too.

That night, after a plain dinner of roast beef and mashed potatoes, Melba served thick chocolate pudding. Everyone agreed that the meal was a great success, compared with what the women had been providing.

Later, while Bonnie was at her desk studying for a French test, Clare ran into the nursery to repeat everything her grandmother had said about the new cook.

"She can't read," Clare said as she began preparing for bed. "Not a single word, Grandmother says. So every day while you and I are in school, Grandmother or Winnie will teach her." Clare stripped off her stockings and wiggled her bare toes. "They'll teach her enough math to keep household accounts and count change at the markets, too."

Bonnie, head bent over her French grammar, muttered, "I hope they teach her what a bathtub is for."

"She's simply awful, isn't she?" Clare said. "Mama said she didn't think Melba had ever had a bath."

Bonnie sat up straight and stretched. "Now we know what happened to her last job."

Clare held her nose elegantly. "Can you imagine what Miss Delaney would say?"

Bonnie laughed. "No, I can't. I don't think she's ever even seen anyone like Melba up close. The maids in the boarding annex are all nice, neat women."

Clare sat cross-legged on her bed with her skirt hitched up and her bloomers showing. "They aren't much older than you, Bonnie. Have you ever wondered what they think about us?"

"I did when I first started school there," Bonnie confessed. "Sometimes I felt embarrassed when I saw them bringing the little girls across the garden from the dormitory annex in the morning. I passed one of them outside the greenhouse once and she said, 'Good morning, miss.' It bothered me that she called me 'miss.' And then I remembered that she knows how to earn a living and I don't, so I almost envied her."

"You wouldn't want to be a maid!" Clare said.

Bonnie remembered the man in the train station on the day she arrived in Seattle. He had offered her some sort of job in a hotel, and she had been willing to consider it until the man at the counter chased him away.

"No," she said slowly. "I wouldn't want to be a maid. But I want to be something."

"Girls like us are never maids," Clare said.

"I wonder why," Bonnie said.

"Because we come from the right families, you idiot," Clare said. She was frowning again.

"A maid could never work any harder than Mama and I did on the farm," Bonnie said. "And later, at Aunt Suze's house, she treated me worse than a maid."

"But you're here now," Clare said. "You don't even have to think about those days."

It had been a while since Bonnie had remembered the endless, backbreaking work on the farm, and then at Aunt Suze's house. She had been worse off than Melba, at least at her aunt's place. But there was a difference, Bonnie knew. She had been raised by an educated mother.

But still, was that the difference between Melba and herself? Or Melba and Clare?

"I forgot to tell you that I saw James Terry this afternoon," Clare said as she pulled off her dress. "He was talking to Grandmother about doing chores here. He's already working for some of the neighbors." She stripped off her petticoat and tossed it on top of her dress.

"Is she going to hire him?" Bonnie asked.

Clare shrugged as she unhooked her corset, a garment required by the Academy—and, strangely enough, by modern Cousin Audra—for all girls past the age of twelve. "I didn't think I should ask. She'd only start in again about my staying outside to talk to him in the dark."

"If he comes to work here, you can sneak down to the basement and talk to him while he's cleaning ashes out of the furnace,'' Bonnie said, suddenly bitter.

"Maybe I will," Clare said as she yanked her nightgown over her head and finished undressing underneath it. "And won't *you* be the jealous one?"

Bonnie didn't answer the question, because she knew she would be jealous. James was what some of the older girls at school would call "divine."

"Melba will take him away from you," Bonnie said.

"Let her try," Clare said. She bounced on her bed. "*I* smell like Florida Water, not dirty underclothes."

"You aren't supposed to use your mother's Florida Water," Bonnie said.

"Nag, nag, nag," Clare said cheerfully. She turned out the lamp beside her bed and rolled over on her side. "Good night, bookworm."

"Good night," Bonnie said shortly. She gritted her teeth. Clare was such a *child*.

Dear Elena:

Cousin Audra has hired James to help with the furnace and do other odd jobs. Clare is very happy. What she doesn't know is that Melba, the cook, is also very happy. Of course, James would never really be interested in someone like her.

On February 6, 1919, the workers in Seattle went on strike and everything came to a halt. The streetcars weren't running, so Mr. Johnson, who never walked to work, tried to call for a taxicab and discovered that the telephone line was dead.

The morning papers had been delivered, and they denounced the strike as a communist holiday. Mr. Partridge and Mr. Nickerson were anxious to get to their offices so they could find out what was happening, hour by

100

hour. They left without having their usual second cups of coffee. Mr. Johnson stormed out with them and slammed the door behind him.

Mr. Younger tapped his way out of the back parlor. "I hope you ladies aren't concerned," he said. "The paper last night predicted riots, but that isn't likely to happen. And the Wobblies wouldn't come this far away from the business district and the waterfront."

"We aren't the least bit concerned," Winnie told him. "Many of the men who belong to the International Workers of the World are the husbands of the women we work with at the neighborhood house. They respect us."

"Still, I don't think the girl—what's her name—Melba. I don't think she should go to the market this morning. It's probably closed anyway. And perhaps someone should walk to school with Bonnie and Clare."

"We had planned to do that," Sally said. "I won't open the library today, out of respect for the union men on strike, so I'll take them."

"You don't look as if you felt very well," Cousin Audra said.

"I'm fine," Sally said.

"You look feverish," Winnie said. "I'll walk the girls to school. Why don't you spend the day in bed, Sally? There's still Spanish flu going around. You can't take chances."

Winnie walked to school with the girls, and the walk was as uneventful as it ever had been. If the general strike was causing problems in Seattle, there was no evidence of it in their quiet neighborhood. Cousin Audra met them when school was over, and told them on the way home that Sally was no better and Winnie had been called away to the neighborhood house, where a crowd of worried women had gathered.

"Should the doctor come to see Mama?" Clare asked. "If it's Spanish flu, she could die."

"She's not that sick, child," Cousin Audra said. But Bonnie could tell how worried she was, so she wasn't surprised when they reached the boarding house and saw for themselves how bad Sally looked.

She was in bed, with extra blankets piled on her, but still she shivered. Her lips were blue. She looked almost as ill as Mrs. Terry had the day she died.

"Maybe we should call the doctor," Cousin Audra said as she tucked one of Sally's blankets securely under the mattress. "It can't hurt for him to look at you."

Sally didn't argue, so Cousin Audra tried to use the telephone, but the line was still dead.

"Someone will have to go around to the doctor's house, I'm afraid," Cousin Audra said. "I'll send Melba for him."

But the new cook refused to go. "I'm not going anywhere when those mobs are running around killing people," she declared.

"I doubt very much if there are mobs running around anywhere," Cousin Audra said sharply. "And no one is killing anyone."

"I won't do it," Melba said, and she turned her back and walked away.

"Heavens," Cousin Audra breathed. "All right, it looks as if I must go myself. Bonnie, can you manage until Winnie gets back?"

"No!" Bonnie cried, alarmed. "I don't know anything about taking care of people who are as sick as Sally. I'll go for the doctor and you stay here in case she needs you."

"I don't think you should go alone," Cousin Audra said.

"If you'd send Melba, then why not send me?" Bonnie argued. "We're the same age."

"But she's—" Cousin Audra began, and then she stopped. Whatever it was that Melba was and Bonnie was not, Cousin Audra was not about to explain it.

"I'll get my coat and leave right now," Bonnie said. "His house is the white one with yellow windowboxes on the last corner before the streetcar starts uphill, isn't it?"

"I don't know if you should go, Bonnie," Cousin Audra said. "This doesn't seem right."

Mr. Younger tapped into the hall. "I'll go with Bonnie," he said.

"But—" Cousin Audra began.

"I would at least be a presence," he said shortly. "I would at least be company for her on what sounds like a very long walk."

Bonnie longed to tell him that he would create more problems than he solved, but she was afraid she would hurt his pride. "I'd be glad if you went with me," she said. "I'll feel much better."

There was a moment of confusion on the porch, when Bonnie wanted to take his arm and he explained that he would rather take hers. "Just tell me when we reach steps and curbs and other things I could fall over," he said. "I'm sure we'll get along very well."

Bonnie doubted it, but she let him take her arm and guided him down the steps. She looked back once, when they were halfway down the block, and saw Cousin Audra and Clare watching them from the porch.

We'll be fine, she told herself.

But she was not so certain of that when they were within several blocks of the doctor's house. A mob surged through the street ahead of them, shouting and waving placards. From a sidestreet, another yelling

103

crowd of men, younger ones, burst out into the intersection.

Mr. Younger stopped. "What's happening?"

Bonnie told him about the two groups of men.

"Who are the ones who aren't carrying signs?" he asked urgently. "Do you think they are Pinkerton detectives?"

Bonnie knew that Seattle businessmen had wanted to hire Pinkerton detectives from back East to come and wait for the strike to begin so that they could break it up. She had read the articles in the paper about them to Mr. Younger. They were said to be more violent than strikers ever were.

"I think they're too young for that," she said hesitantly. "Some of them are wearing sweaters with University of Washington letters on them. Oh. They're fraternity boys. Now I see that some of them are carrying signs, too. They have their Greek letters on them."

"Smart alecks," Mr. Younger muttered savagely. "They think they're clever fellows, coming out to help break up the strike."

The two mobs met and tangled. Men shouted curses and threats. Someone screamed.

Mr. Younger's grip tightened on Bonnie's arm. "We can't just stand here," he said. "We have to get off the sidewalk. Tell me what's around us. Quickly."

"There are houses here, and small yards—"

"Is anyone looking out? Is there someone you could ask for help?"

As Bonnie watched, a curtain on the house closest to them twitched back. "Someone's looking out. Should I try to get their attention?"

"Yes. Let's go up to the door. I can't let you stay out here when anything might happen."

It was impossible to tell the fighting men apart as they

struggled together in the street. Several uniformed men on horseback plunged into the crowd, and more men screamed.

"Bonnie! You must get off the sidewalk!" Mr. Younger cried.

"Come," she said. "We'll ask the people in the house if we can stay on the porch." She led him as far as the bottom step and then ran up alone. But no one answered when she knocked, and the curtain had fallen back into place.

"They won't help," she told him when she went back down the steps. "They won't even answer the door."

Hoofs rang on the pavement. Several men lay bleeding in the street now.

"There's a path between the houses," Bonnie said. "It must lead to an alley. We'll go back there."

She led him between the houses, to a trash-strewn alley, and hurried him along the rough, muddy track.

"I'm afraid I'll lose my way to the doctor's house if we walk in the alleys," she said. "But the street is too dangerous."

"Then let's stop here and wait," he said.

His face was pale, and he seemed to be straining to hear.

A gun went off, and Mr. Younger flinched and stumbled against her. "Oh god," he said. "Are you all right, Bonnie?"

"We've got to find a place to hide," she said.

"I never should have let you come here," he said.

"It was my idea," she said. "If you hadn't come with me, I'd be alone now. Here's a shed, and the door's open. We'll wait inside until they go away. But poor Sally. What will Cousin Audra do when we don't come back with the doctor?"

"We'll bring him back," Mr. Younger said.

But darkness fell, and they were still hiding in the small shed several blocks from the doctor's house, while the riot raged on.

Once someone on horseback rode down the alley. Another time, several men ran through it, shouting unintelligibly. Bonnie could smell smoke, and through the cracks in the rough board walls, she saw a red glow reflected off the smoke hovering over the city.

Mr. Younger slipped his arm around her shoulders. "Don't be afraid," he said. "It can't last much longer, and then we'll go on our way."

"It's like a war," Bonnie said, her voice cracking.

He was silent for a long time, and then he said, "No. We have the hope of accomplishing what we started out to do before this evening is over. In a war, there's no hope at all."

9

*S*huddering with cold, they waited in the shed for better than an hour, and when at last the men's voices died away, they made their halting way down the alley.

"I think I should take you back home," Bonnie said as they crossed the intersection. "It's cold enough to snow."

Mr. Younger was silent for a moment, and then he said, "Maybe I should take *you* home."

She realized she had offended him, but he wasn't facing the truth of the situation. He was at home in the dark, but he knew nothing about the neighborhood, and there was no possibility of his finding his way alone. Or leading her anywhere.

"We'll go to the doctor's house," she said. "Step up here—we're at the curb. It's not much farther."

At the doctor's house, no one answered Bonnie's knock for several minutes. She knew someone was home, because she heard a child crying shrilly upstairs, so she knocked over and over until at last a woman answered.

"Audra Devereaux sent me," Bonnie said. "Her daughter is very ill and needs the doctor."

"He's at the hospital, taking care of people who were injured tonight," the woman said. "I don't know when he'll be back."

"Our telephone doesn't work," Bonnie explained. "If yours is working, would you call and ask him to come when he's through at the hospital?"

"Ours doesn't work, either," the woman said. Upstairs, the child cried louder, and the woman began easing the door shut.

"I'm sorry I can't help you," she said. "I don't know when I'll see my husband, but when he comes home, I'll tell him you need him. Now, please, my baby has an earache and I must take care of him."

The door clicked shut quietly.

"What should we do?" Bonnie asked. "Maybe if we get her back and ask her what hospital he's working in, we could go there and talk to him."

"I doubt if that would do any good," Mr. Younger said. "Between the flu and the strike, the hospitals must be busy. Your family will be worried about you. And we should tell them that the doctor can't come right away."

They began the long climb up the hill, walking as quickly as they could on the deserted streets. Every house they passed was dark, but Bonnie felt eyes were watching her from behind curtains as their footsteps clacked along the icy sidewalks. No dogs barked at them. No automobiles passed.

"What are you wearing?" Mr. Younger asked suddenly.

"Why?" she asked, astonished.

"Sometimes I need to know small things like that," he said quietly. "Sometimes I am desperate to know."

"I'm wearing my school coat," she said. "It's dark blue and has brass buttons. I'm wearing my school hat,

108

too. And my uniform—a jacket and a pleated skirt. My blouse is white, with a black ribbon bow. My shoes are black.''

"Do you like wearing a uniform?"

"Yes," she confessed. "I like it when people can tell that I'm a student at the Academy."

He laughed. "And when will you graduate?"

"A year from this June," she said.

"Then what will you do?" he asked.

"Why, I'll go to the university. Be careful now, Mr. Younger. The sidewalk is uneven here."

He stumbled a little and recovered. "What will you study in the university?" he asked.

"I don't know yet," she said, puzzled by his curiosity. "Sometimes I think I'd like to be a teacher. That's what my mother planned to do, but she married my father instead. I could be a librarian. Or a nurse."

"What if you wanted to be a doctor?" he asked. "What would she think of that?"

"A doctor?" she asked. She shook her head. "There isn't a medical school here. I never even thought of being a doctor."

"What?" he asked. "A young Suffragette like yourself never considered that? Tell me the truth, Bonnie. What do you see yourself doing in ten years?"

"I can't think that far ahead," she said.

"Try."

She guided him off a curb, across the street, and up another curb. "I suppose I'll end up being a teacher. That's what most women do when they finish college. Or they get married and don't do anything at all outside their homes."

"You'd like that?"

She considered this, then said, "No."

"So you don't want to be like Mrs. Devereaux and Winnie?"

"Of course I want to be like them!" she said. "They are wonderful. I want to be exactly like them."

"But they can't see that their volunteer work doesn't mean much if their attempts to teach women to be independent don't extend as far as themselves," he said.

"They *are* independent," she insisted. "They support themselves."

"By waiting on men," he said.

"I hate this conversation!" she said. "You're getting me all mixed up."

"No, you were already mixed up, but you didn't know it," he said.

"I don't like hearing you say anything bad about my family," she said.

He laughed quietly. "I adore the women in your house," he said. "They are charming and intelligent and witty."

"But you're saying they can't take care of themselves very well," she argued.

"Yes. That's what I'm saying."

"Don't say it again," Bonnie told him. "I don't want to hear it. What about you? Why aren't you learning to read in Braille? There's a school downtown for blind people that teaches it, and it's free. If it's so important for people to take care of themselves, why don't you learn to read?"

She hadn't meant to say so much. She wanted to defend the women in her family from Mr. Younger's sharp criticism, but she'd had no right to attack him.

"I'm sorry!" she blurted when he didn't speak. "I shouldn't have said anything."

He cleared his throat. "Where did you learn about this school?"

"Our teacher took us there a few weeks ago so we could see what it's like," she said.

"And did your teacher also take you to the zoo?" he asked.

Bonnie burst into tears. "I hate the way you twist things around. You hurt people's feelings. I'm sorry you're blind. I wish I could do something to help you. But you don't have a right to punish the rest of us."

"I wasn't aware that I was doing that," he said stiffly. He loosened his grip on her arm.

"If you let go of me, you'll fall," she cried. "Don't be stupid. Heroes can fall down and break their bones just like everybody else."

"Whatever gave you the ridiculous idea that I was a hero?" he asked.

"Well . . ." she began. And then she stopped. He must realize that she called him that because he had been injured in the war.

"Being blind doesn't make me a hero," he said. "I lost my sight because I was fool enough to want to be brave in the eyes of the men around me."

Footsteps hurried toward them in the dark, and both of them stopped. Then she saw Winnie run into the circle of light cast by a street lamp.

"Winnie!" Bonnie cried.

"Oh, here you are!" Winnie gasped as she reached them. "We've been worried sick. I was heading for the doctor's house to see if you'd ever reached it."

"He's not there," Mr. Younger said. "He's working at a hospital tonight. But his wife said she'll tell him about Sally as soon as she sees him."

"How is Sally?" Bonnie asked quickly.

"She's very ill," Winnie said. "Mrs. Nelson—you know Marietta's mother, Bonnie—she brought over the last of the medicine the doctor had given her husband

111

when he had Spanish flu. She swears it helped him, but Sally doesn't seem to be responding to it.''

"It's too soon," Mr. Younger said. "People don't respond to medication right away."

"Mr. Younger knows about these things," Bonnie told Winnie. "He once planned to be a doctor, like his father."

"Then, we mustn't be discouraged," Winnie said. She took Mr. Younger's arm, but he explained that he would rather hold hers, and the two of them turned toward home.

Bonnie trailed behind, wiping tears from her eyes. Did Mr. Younger really know anything about medicine, or was he merely trying to reassure them?

Cousin Audra waited for them in the dining room. She had persuaded the reluctant Melba to prepare a platter of sandwiches. A pot of soup simmered on the back of the wood stove.

Winnie told her that the doctor wasn't coming that night. Cousin Audra nodded.

"Then we'll manage by ourselves," she said. "Mr. Partridge sent a note by his assistant to let us know that he and Mr. Nickerson were spending the night at their club. They didn't want to be out on the streets after dark. We haven't heard from Mr. Johnson, but he probably decided to do the same. I wish you'd look in on Sally, Bonnie. She might still be awake. When she asked for you earlier, I had to tell her you weren't back yet, and she was very worried."

"We almost got caught by the strikers and the men fighting them," Bonnie said. "We hid in a shack in an alley until they all went away." As she remembered her fear, her hands trembled and she couldn't unbutton her coat.

"Darling, let me help you off with your coat and hat," Cousin Audra said. "There now. Run upstairs to see if

112

Sally's awake, and then come down for something to eat. You must join us, too, Mr. Younger. Hot soup will be good for you."

"If it would be possible to have a tray in my room, I would be very grateful," Mr. Younger said. His voice was cool and restrained, but Bonnie swung around to look at him.

"Are you all right?" she asked.

"I'm a little tired," he said. He tapped toward the stairs, one hand outstretched. "If I could have that tray, Mrs. Devereaux . . ."

"I'll bring it up myself," Cousin Audra said. She looked questioningly at Bonnie.

"Good night, Mr. Younger," Bonnie said. "Thank you for going with me."

Mr. Younger didn't reply.

Clare passed him as she ran downstairs. "I thought I heard you," she told Bonnie. "Is the doctor coming? Why did you take so long?"

Before Bonnie could tell the story again, Cousin Audra broke in and explained. Clare scowled at Bonnie.

"I would have found the doctor," she said.

"And he would have refused to come," Winnie said briskly. "Clare, shouldn't you be getting ready for bed? It's very late."

"I want to stay up and see how Mama gets along," Clare said stubbornly.

"Clare," Cousin Audra said flatly.

"Oh, all right!" Clare cried. She pounded back upstairs, and Bonnie followed slowly, as far as the second floor.

Perhaps she and Mr. Younger should have walked downtown and tried to find the doctor, or another one. If Sally grew worse overnight, it would be their fault because they gave up too soon.

Bonnie found Sally awake but groggy and she sat down beside her bed in a cushioned rocker. "How are you?" she asked, dreading the answer.

"I believe that vile-tasting medicine Mrs. Nelson brought over is beginning to help me," Sally said hoarsely. She coughed violently for nearly a minute and shook her head helplessly.

"I'll let you get your rest," Bonnie said as she got up to leave. "I'm sorry we couldn't bring the doctor back."

"He'll come tomorrow," Sally said. "How did Mr. Younger manage the long walk? Audra told me he insisted on going with you."

"He did better than I thought he could," Bonnie said. She considered telling Sally about the mobs of men that frightened them, and decided to save the story for another time. She smoothed Sally's hair back from her hot forehead and smiled at her. "Everything will be better tomorrow," she whispered as Sally's eyes closed drowsily.

Clare hissed at her over the third floor banister when she left the room. "Is Mama awake?"

"She's falling asleep now," Bonnie said. "I think she's better."

"You were alone with Mr. Younger for a long time," Clare said. "What did you talk about?"

"Nothing that mattered," Bonnie said.

What would Cousin Audra say, she wondered, if she ever found out how cruel I was to Mr. Younger? I shouldn't have lashed out at him. All he had done was try to encourage me to be more self-reliant.

But how dare he, when he had turned himself into a hermit?

Cousin Audra passed her in the hall, carrying a tray

for Mr. Younger. She looked exhausted, but her hair was neat and her dress immaculate.

"Winnie's in the kitchen," Cousin Audra said. "She'll serve your soup, since Melba has gone to bed."

"Is Melba sick?" Bonnie asked.

Cousin Audra laughed. "No. She said all she is being paid to do is fix our meals, not keep them warm for hours and feed us when we finally decide to eat."

"What?" Bonnie cried.

Cousin Audra was halfway up the stairs. "Winnie and I must spend more time with her, explaining things," she said.

Why? Bonnie wondered. From what she had heard, Melba was showing no signs of learning to read. Lessons in good manners seemed a waste of time.

She ate at the kitchen table and helped Winnie clear away the leftovers. By the time she started upstairs to the nursery, the hall clock was striking eleven.

She could hear Sally coughing through the vent in the floor all night long.

The doctor arrived the next day while Bonnie and Clare were in school. By the time they got home, Sally was feeling better and sitting up, drinking tea.

"He said it's a light case of Spanish flu," Sally told the girls. "I felt so bad last night that I thought I'd die. If this is a light case, I'm glad I didn't have a bad one."

"When can you get out of bed?" Clare asked.

"In a few days, he said," Sally told her.

"But he's sure you're going to be all right," Clare said.

"He was certain," Sally said.

"I wish Mr. Johnson had the flu instead of you," Clare said.

"We'd better let your mother rest," Bonnie said, and

she took Clare by the arm and led her to the door.

"Heavens!" she said when they were out of Sally's hearing. "Never say anything like that. Wouldn't you feel terrible if Mr. Johnson got sick? You don't want to wish anything on anybody."

"Well, he wouldn't get sick because of anything I said, Bonnie!" Clare cried. "I'd have to tie a paper strip on the Ornament Tree for something like that to happen."

Bonnie laughed until she nearly cried.

"It's not funny!" Clare said. "Things really do come true if you write them down and tie the note to the tree. I've had it happen to me. I wanted my father to come home, and he did."

"And you despise him," Bonnie pointed out.

"Oh, well," Clare said, scowling. "At least he came home."

"Don't put another note on the tree about him unless you ask your mother first," Bonnie advised. "I don't think she was happy to see him."

Clare ran ahead of Bonnie, and darted into the back parlor where Mr. Younger was sitting. "The newspaper is here already," Bonnie heard her say. "I'll read it to you now, if you like."

She hates reading to him, Bonnie thought. She's doing this to spite me.

"Read the strike news to me, Clare," Mr. Younger said.

Something in Bonnie's chest hurt, as if she had received a blow. Mr. Younger was still angry with her. Why else would he want Clare to read to him instead of her?

Clare shot her a triumphant look when she came back to the hall for one of the newspapers on the table. Bonnie did her best to act as if she didn't care, and went to the

116

pantry to take down china to set the dining room table.

How many would be there? Perhaps Melba knew.

She pushed through the swinging door to the kitchen. The back door stood open, and Melba leaned against the frame, talking to James Terry.

Both of them looked guilty when they heard Bonnie come in.

"What do *you* want?" Melba asked bluntly.

Bonnie's face burned. "Do you know how many will be here for dinner? I'm going to set the table now."

"How should I know?" Melba said with her irritating smirk.

"Didn't anyone tell you how many to cook for?" Bonnie asked.

"I'm cooking for everybody, just like I always do," Melba said. "Eat or don't eat. I don't care." Her smirk implied that Bonnie's question was somehow ridiculous.

"Since you can't count, how do you know how many 'everybody' is?" Bonnie snapped. She turned her back on them and left the kitchen.

They laughed, both of them. Bonnie was so angry that her hands trembled while she took down the plates.

How can Melba laugh at what I said? she wondered. Now James knows she can't read. Why isn't she embarrassed?

Mr. Nickerson and Mr. Partridge reached the house by sunset, filled with news of the city brought to a stop by the strike. Mr. Johnson arrived a few minutes later, furious.

"We'll break their backs!" he declared. "You'll see. We'll stop this strike and all they'll get for their trouble is fired."

While Bonnie helped carry food from the kitchen, she carefully avoided making eye contact with Melba. The girl's maddening smirk wouldn't be easy to forget. And neither would knowing that handsome James had laughed at her. She remembered how much time she had spent thinking about him, wondering about him. What a waste of time.

After dinner, Cousin Audra asked Bonnie if she could speak to her privately for a moment in the nursery. Clare was sitting with her mother, reading a novel aloud. The boarders, afraid to go downtown for their after-dinner drinks, played bridge in the front parlor with Winnie. Mr. Younger sat in the dark in the back parlor.

Bonnie climbed the stairs with Cousin Audra, wondering what she had to say that needed privacy. Her conversation with Melba didn't cross her mind.

"Let's sit down, dear," Cousin Audra said, and she took the chair beside Clare's bed. Bonnie sat on her own chair.

"What is it?" she asked.

"Melba told me a regrettable story a few minutes ago in the kitchen," Cousin Audra said. "I hope it isn't true. Did you accuse her of not being able to count?"

"Well, she can't," Bonnie said defensively.

"Yes, and she knows it better than anyone else. It wasn't necessary for you to point it out, especially since our new handyman was there."

Bonnie blinked back tears. "I'm sorry," she said, although she wasn't. "But she was so rude to me."

Cousin Audra smiled gently. "Young women in your position don't answer rudeness with more rudeness," she said. "No matter how much we are tempted, we never belittle the people who serve us."

Bonnie folded her hands in her lap and stared down at them, humiliated. Her mother had told her not to bicker with the help when she caught Bonnie arguing fiercely with the young man who helped in the barn. Why hadn't she learned the lesson then?

"Now there's one other thing, my sweet," Cousin

Audra said. "What did you say to Mr. Younger about the school for the blind?"

Bonnie looked up and blurted guiltily, "Is he angry with me, too?"

Cousin Audra laughed. "No, certainly not. He said you had suggested that he consider learning Braille there. His mother had told me that she tried many times to persuade him to learn, but he always refused. I only wondered what magic you worked on him. He asked me to show him the way to the school and help him make arrangements. It was wonderful of you to take an interest in him, Bonnie. I'm sure he'll be grateful for the rest of his life."

Bonnie's heart thumped painfully. "Then he wasn't angry at what I said?"

"No, no."

Bonnie sighed with relief. Should she confess that she and Mr. Younger had been shouting at each other in the street? No. If he hadn't told, then she wouldn't. He was a gentleman.

But Melba had better look out, Bonnie thought. Out of respect for Cousin Audra, she wouldn't say another rude word, no matter how much the girl provoked her. But Mr. Joshua, her mother's lawyer, had told her something once when she had been upset about the way Aunt Suze had treated her.

"Whatever people do, good or bad, comes back to them seven times," the old man had said. "I don't think Suze will live long enough to collect all the hard times she's got coming to her. It might get your mind off your troubles if you start counting hers."

Dear Elena:

I wish I didn't talk so much.

10

⊲⊳⊹⊱⊰

The general strike lasted five days. Each evening at dinner, Mr. Partridge and Mr. Nickerson discussed what they had seen and heard downtown—the rallies and speeches, the confrontations between union workers and their opponents, and the increasing frustration of the people who only wanted to do their work in peace.

Mr. Johnson made a point of contradicting everything the other diners said, no matter what it was. It seemed to Bonnie that sometimes he contradicted himself.

Mr. Younger, from his sanctuary in the back parlor, added his own savage opinions, which always enraged Mr. Johnson. Cousin Audra's peacemaking skills were strained.

"The women in this house must do something to restore sanity to the dinner hour," Cousin Audra told Bonnie and Clare one afternoon.

They were talking in the bedroom Cousin Audra shared with Sally. One corner had been turned into sitting room, and the girls sat side by side on a small red velvet sofa.

"What can we do about it?" Clare demanded. "The boarders are so boring I don't even listen."

"I thought we might plan ahead to introduce a few subjects they can't quarrel over,' Cousin Audra said. "There are all sorts of interesting articles in the newspapers. For instance, we could talk about the possibility of liquor being outlawed soon."

Bonnie had to look away. She was afraid Cousin Audra would read her face correctly and know she was struggling with laughter. Everyone in the house knew that Cousin Audra deeply regretted the men's taste for after-dinner drinks, even though she was never rude enough to mention it to them.

Sally, propped up in bed with a cup of tea, burst out laughing in spite of an obvious battle to hold it in. "There's an idea to calm them down! They'll have fits if they're reminded that they might have to give up those after-dinner drinks. No, Mother, Prohibition is not a good subject to bring up. You give them more credit than they deserve."

"Show them the new birth-control pamphlets you had printed, Grandmother," Clare said bitterly. "As soon as they find out you and Winnie are going to start handing them out again—and downtown by the library this time!—they'll all move out. Well, Mr. Younger won't. We'll have him here for the rest of our lives, making fun of us and yelling things from the back parlor that nobody understands and everybody resents."

"Clare, you aren't helping matters with that attitude," Sally said.

"Mama, you don't know what it's been like in the dining room since you got sick!" Clare cried. "The men argue—or rather, Mr. Johnson and Mr. Younger argue—and Winnie swells up and turns purple because she's trying so hard to keep from contradicting them. And out in the kitchen, that nasty Melba is throwing pots and pans around and singing things she must be learning in the burlesque theater. Why do we keep her? Why do we keep any of them?''

"You're upset because James Terry hangs around the kitchen talking to her," Cousin Audra said. "I've explained to her that it's not suitable. She'll come around to our way of thinking when she sees there are nicer ways of doing things."

Bonnie laughed shortly, said, "Sorry, Cousin Audra," and covered her mouth to keep back another burst of laughter. Melba would come around to Cousin Audra's proper ways about the same time Mr. Johnson would stop calling Mr. Younger a spoiled rich-boy union booster and a communist traitor.

Winnie, who perched on the foot of Sally's bed, said, "Audra and I thought you girls might help us smooth things over. Whenever we begin a pleasant subject, please try to add your thoughts on it. You're old enough to be gracious."

"I don't have any thoughts on *anything* people talk about at dinner," Clare said.

"You want to see the new play at the Metropolitan," Bonnie said. "Why don't we talk about it?"

"Thank you, Bonnie," Cousin Audra said. "That's a good idea. We can discuss the play tonight."

"For the whole meal?" Clare asked. "Nobody wants to talk about a play for a whole meal, and meanwhile, out in the kitchen, Melba will be slinging pans against the wall and singing, 'They Go Wild, Simply Wild, Over Me,' and 'Soldier Boy.' "

"Oh, help," Winnie said, laughing.

"It's not funny!" Clare said. "It's disgusting! Everybody at school knows we have boarders, and that's bad enough. But our boarders are all crazy, and our cook won't take a bath and she picks her teeth and—Mama, stop laughing! You should see her after she leaves the house to go to the market! She unbuttons the top of her blouse clear down to you-know-where and sticks out her chest. And she's doesn't wear a corset—or even a brassiere like Winnie does. Isn't that so, Bonnie?''

Bonnie, still suffering from the embarrassing conversation she'd had with Cousin Audra about Melba, merely shrugged. But everything Clare had said was true. Melba was outrageous. However, she could cook, and she was willing to work for what Cousin Audra could pay. No one else was.

That night, Sally came down to dinner for the first time since she became ill. Dutifully, Winnie introduced the subject of the new play at the Metropolitan. Cousin Audra asked if the girls were interested in going to the matinee on Saturday. Sally suggested they wait a week until she was well enough to go, because she didn't want to miss it. The men all listened with apparent interest.

In the kitchen, a pan hit the sink. The tinkle of broken glass followed. Melba sang off-key. '' 'Everybody's doin' it, doin' it, doin' it.' ''

"My wife enjoyed matinees," Mr. Nickerson said wistfully as he buttered a slice of bread.

"She had her own box, as I remember," Cousin Audra said with gentle determination. "What a lovely lady."

'' 'Everybody's doin' it,' '' bellowed Melba as she kept time tapping a spoon on what sounded like an empty bucket.

"Lovely, yes," Mr. Nickerson said, meaning his dead wife.

'' 'Doin' it, doin' it,' '' Melba sang. The swinging door from the pantry burst open and Melba, smelling strongly of onions and perspiration, said, "Anybody want seconds on the spuds?"

"Oh, dear," Cousin Audra breathed. She straightened

herself and looked around the table. "Potatoes, anyone? No? Thank you, Melba, but no one wants another helping."

"Suit yourself," Melba said, and she disappeared back into the kitchen.

Bonnie was certain she heard James's soft laughter in the kitchen, and she nearly choked on her jealousy. Why did he find Melba attractive? Once he had asked Bonnie to walk around the block with him. What would have happened if she had?

Mr. Younger tapped his spoon on his glass. Clare pretended great interest in cutting a tiny piece off her slice of roast beef. Bonnie sighed to herself and got to her feet.

"What's going on out there?" Mr. Younger demanded when she walked into the back parlor.

"What do you mean?" Bonnie asked.

"Why all this conversation about the play?"

"I thought you liked talking about plays," she said.

"You aren't talking about the play to be talking about the play," he said rather incomprehensibly. "You're deliberately *not* talking about other things."

"Oh!" Now she understood. Mr. Younger had not been fooled by Cousin Audra's attempt to keep peace in the dining room. But could she explain this to Mr. Younger? That might be dangerous. Knowing him as well as she did, she felt certain he would find a way to ridicule their efforts to avoid controversy.

"Maybe they're all tired tonight," she said innocently.

"Ha," Mr. Younger muttered. "Have the evening papers come?"

"Yes. Do you want Clare to come in and read to you now?"

"No. I want you to read to me. I miss you."

"The headline says the strike is over," Bonnie said. "You and the others can go downtown for your after-dinner drinks. Wouldn't you like that better?"

Mr. Younger cocked his head. "I like what you like," he said. "Sit down and talk to me."

She sat on the chair across the table from him. "What do you want to talk about?"

"Have you given any thought to the conversation we had on the night of our great adventure?"

Bewildered, she said, "We talked about many things."

"We spoke of your going to the university and what you plan to study," he said. "Have you been thinking about it?"

"No," she said frankly. She had fallen into a pleasant routine at home and at school, one day at a time, like the women in the house.

He sighed. "Bonnie. Please listen. Consider how far you can reach, and then set your goal beyond that."

"I don't know what you mean," she said, although she had understood him perfectly. The conversation made her uneasy. What did he expect of her?

"Run along, then," he said. "I'll shed my wisdom on the talented Miss Melba after this. I suspect that she is more ambitious than you. Although she doesn't sing nearly as well."

"You heard her?" Bonnie asked, embarrassed.

"Who didn't hear her?" he said. He grinned. "I'd be interested in learning where she picks these things up."

"The same place . . ." Bonnie Rose began, and then she stopped. Cousin Audra's admonition rang in her mind.

Mr. Younger laughed for a long time. "Oh, Bonnie, what would I do if I didn't have you to make me laugh?" He got to his feet. "I'll see if the other men

125

are ready for their first night out in nearly a week. You're relieved of your duty to me this evening, young lady.''

He was halfway to the door when she said, ''Is it true that you might learn Braille?''

He didn't answer, but went through the doorway and disappeared.

Dear Elena:

Clare was thirteen on Valentine's Day. To celebrate, Cousin Audra and Sally gave her a luncheon party in a downtown restaurant, and her whole class from the academy was invited.

I'm certain they couldn't afford the extravagance. A few days before, I answered the back door when the grocer came to ask for payment on the bill. He and I both were so embarrassed.

Cousin Audra refuses to accept money from Mr. Joshua for my expenses, even though my allowance from the estate could settle many of the accounts she owes. Mr. Younger tried to pay her more for his board and room, but she refused.

Cousin Audra and Winnie don't worry about anything, so I worry for them.

Clare's party was a great success, though.

One afternoon in March, Winnie came home from the neighborhood house with a disturbing story for Cousin Audra. Bonnie and Clare had been working on school assignments in the nursery, and could hear everything that was said through the grate in the floor that let heat into their room.

''A woman came in after you left,'' Winnie told Cousin Audra. ''She's a housekeeper, but she's eager to learn office skills, and I think we might be able to work out a plan for part-time instruction. But that's not what I want to tell you.''

"You look upset," Cousin Audra said.

"You're not going to believe this," Winnie said.

It was at that point that the girls upstairs began actively eavesdropping.

"Remember when we met Mr. Johnson, and he told us his wife was in a mental hospital?"

"I remember," Cousin Audra said. "Tragic."

"The woman who came in today—Miss Schiller—was working for the Johnsons when it happened," Winnie said. "She'd been there a few months but didn't like it. Mrs. Johnson, she said, was very nice but quite timid, and no wonder. Mr. Johnson abused her terribly, and even in front of Miss Schiller. The money was all Mrs. Johnson's. She had inherited it from her parents, but Mr. Johnson took control of it. The laws allow it. She wanted to divorce him for many reasons, and if she did, she'd also get back control of her inheritance. She actually left him once, and went to stay in a hotel. He and his lawyer hired men to take her out of the hotel and put her in the mental hospital for observation. There was a court hearing, but she wasn't told about it so she couldn't hire a lawyer to tell her side of things. Miss Schiller doesn't know what went on in the court, but the judge declared Mrs. Johnson insane and ordered her committed. Mr. Johnson was made her guardian.''

"And now he's got all her money," Cousin Audra said.

"Not only that," Winnie said. "The house was her family's, but he's sold it and taken all that money, too.''

"And she's still in the asylum?"

"This is the ugliest part," Winnie said. "Miss Schiller went there to see her—she felt so sorry for her—and

127

she was told by a friend who works there that she can't have visitors. The friend says that even people who aren't very disturbed when they get there go mad soon because the conditions are so terrible.''

"You aren't saying that Mrs. Johnson is in a state institution!" Cousin Audra exclaimed.

"He didn't want to waste money on a private hospital," Winnie said. "The state hospitals are worse than prisons."

Clare and Bonnie exchanged a long look.

"I telephoned Mr. Ross as soon as she left," Winnie went on.

Mr. Ross was Cousin Audra's lawyer, Bonnie knew.

"Can he help?" Cousin Audra asked.

"Not really," Winnie said. "He said the law is unfair, but there's nothing that can be done unless the hospital goes to court and says that she is well enough to be released—and they'll never do that. They get money from the state for every patient. Why would they let one of them go?"

"But someone outside must be able to help her," Cousin Audra said.

"It would be very difficult. Mr. Johnson is her next of kin, and he has all the rights. Mr. Ross told me about another woman who was put in the same institution because she argued with the minister in her church. And another one is there because she argued with her doctor."

"I don't believe this," Cousin Audra said. "But I know you're telling me the truth."

"I don't want him here," Winnie said. "I know it's your house, but he is an offense to everything we stand for."

"I'll take care of it," Cousin Audra said. "I will enjoy taking care of it."

Bonnie heard Cousin Audra's door open and close.

"What do you suppose she's going to do?" Bonnie asked Clare.

Clare grinned. "I don't know, but I wish I could watch. Now if she'd only get rid of Melba."

"She won't," Bonnie said. "She's sure she can make Melba over."

"Melba should be grateful that Grandmother is trying to help her," Clare said. "But I'm sure she laughs at Grandmother behind our backs. She and that James Terry. I don't know why I wasted my time on him. He's really quite stupid, you know."

Mr. Johnson did not eat with them again. The girls caught only one more glimpse of him, and that was on Sunday afternoon when he brought a younger man to the house to move his belongings out of the room he had been renting. The other boarders made no comment about his absence, but the arguments at the table stopped.

"Are you going to get another boarder?" Bonnie asked Cousin Audra.

"Certainly," she said. "I'll be more careful next time, though. I hope we've all learned a lesson from this. We can't be too quick to make excuses for people. People must be held accountable for their behavior."

Then what about Melba? Bonnie longed to ask.

On a warm Saturday in March, Cousin Audra asked Bonnie to accompany her downtown while she introduced Mr. Younger to the people at the school that taught Braille.

"He's really going to learn it?" Bonnie asked.

"He's looking into it," Cousin Audra said. "That's the most we can hope for now. But at least it's a start.

I'd like you to come along because I think you give him courage.''

The following Saturday, Mr. Younger was silent on the streetcar as it carried them downtown. Bonnie longed to ask him if he was excited at the prospect of learning to read Braille, but his expression was so forbidding that she kept silent.

The streets were crowded with window shoppers enjoying the warm weather, and Cousin Audra kept close watch on Mr. Younger. Bonnie walked behind them, far enough back so that she wouldn't step on Mr. Younger's heels.

A streetcar clanged its way along the street next to them. Suddenly Bonnie saw a young woman in a shabby blue coat step off the curb and walk directly into the path of the streetcar.

What is she doing? Bonnie thought.

In almost the same instant, the streetcar ran the woman down and passed over her. Several people shouted and rushed toward her, and Bonnie couldn't see anything except their backs.

"What's happened?" Mr. Younger cried. "What's wrong? Why is everyone screaming?"

"A woman walked out in front of the streetcar," Cousin Audra said. "Mr. Younger, I'm going to guide you closer to the buildings. We're in the way of the crowd."

"What happened to the woman?" Mr. Younger asked.

"I can't see her now," Cousin Audra said in a calm, even voice. "Bonnie, are you all right?"

Bonnie was speechless with horror. She had seen the streetcar hit the woman and run over her body, and she knew she must be dead.

Cousin Audra looked back when Bonnie didn't answer. "Oh dear," she said. "Mr. Younger, stand right here and don't move."

She put her arms around Bonnie and drew her close to Mr. Younger. "Take a deep breath, Bonnie. Try not to think about it. There's a tea shop up ahead. We'll go in and have tea and you'll feel better. It's always so hard to see an accident happen."

"It wasn't an accident," Bonnie said. "I saw her walk in front of the streetcar deliberately. I saw her do it."

"No, darling, no. You're mistaken." Cousin Audra took Bonnie by one arm and Mr. Younger with the other. "Come along, my dears. Hot tea is exactly what we need."

Mr. Younger's face was pale and he seemed to be straining to hear what was going on behind them. A mob of people overflowed the street. People were still screaming. Customers streamed out of the shops to shout, "What's going on? What happened?"

"Here's the tea shop," Cousin Audra said. "There's a small incline here, Mr. Younger. Now here's the door."

As soon as the shop door shut behind them, the sounds of the mob were muffled. The air was fragrant with hot tea and toast.

Cousin Audra spoke quietly to a woman in a black uniform, who led them to a table in the back.

"This is a perfect place," she said. "Mr. Younger, let me help you. Bonnie, sit here, please. Would you read the menu to Mr. Younger? They have several kinds of tea and he'll want to hear all the choices."

Bonnie's mind was nearly blank. The bloody death in the street horrified her. The atmosphere in the quiet tea shop was so totally different that it, too, was a shock.

"Did she commit suicide?" Mr. Younger asked harshly.

131

"We can't know what really happened," Cousin Audra said before Bonnie could answer. "We can't change anything, either. So let us sit here and let go of everything that is distressing, all those things we can't control. Let us concentrate on what is happening here and now. Bonnie, please read the menu."

Obediently, Bonnie picked up the menu and read the list of teas. But Mr. Younger didn't listen.

"Order anything for me," he said. He was agitated and scowling. "I don't care what kind of tea I have."

"Mr. Younger," Cousin Audra said. "Help me bring peace and quiet to this moment, please, for Bonnie's sake."

Bonnie's head snapped up. She could manage! There was nothing wrong with her!

She saw Mr. Younger straighten his shoulders and compose himself. "Did I hear you say they have green tea with lemon grass, Bonnie? I'll have that."

"That's what Winnie likes best," Cousin Audra said. "Isn't this a pleasant place? And it's close to your school, Mr. Younger. You could come here for lunch."

Bonnie saw the strain on Cousin Audra's face, the deeper lines, the pale lips. But she has turned this moment around, Bonnie thought. It's what Mama could do. And I'll learn how, too. I'll be like them.

"Do you want butterscotch cookies, Mr. Younger?" she asked him evenly, although her heart was still hammering under her ribs. "I know they're your favorite, and I see them listed on the menu."

"By all means," he said. He smiled, and she thought again how handsome he was, even though he was blind.

But his hands trembled slightly, and she knew that Cousin Audra's magic had not worked so well on him.

From outside, they heard the faint clang of an ambulance bell. It sounded very far away.

Mr. Younger heard it, too, and he sighed.

11

⊰⊹⊱

April came, and along with it, Bonnie's fifteenth birthday. She flatly refused to accept Cousin Audra's plans for a party like Clare's.

"I wish you wouldn't," she told her family. They had gathered in Cousin Audra's room again, in the sitting area in the corner. "It doesn't seem right, with Mama not dead a year yet. And last year, she gave me a party. I'd be thinking about that all the time. I don't believe I can do this."

"Sorry!" Cousin Audra said. "How could I be so thoughtless! We'll have a small family party here, then. Your birthday is on a Saturday, so we'll plan it for the afternoon. The boarders are usually away from the house then." She was mending a tablecloth, and paused to snap off a thread. "We'll have a lovely cake . . ."

"You aren't expecting Melba to bake the cake, are you?" Clare scoffed. "She bakes horrible cakes, and she probably wouldn't even try to make one for Bonnie. Or me, either. She hates us."

Sally sighed. "Don't start in on that again, Clare. She doesn't hate you. But you must see that she might feel a little resentment toward you and Bonnie. After all,

133

she's just a girl, too, but she has no advantages at all.''

"Nobody made her be our cook," Clare said.

"She doesn't have a family," Winnie said. "She didn't have anywhere to go. As soon as she learns some office skills, she'll find a good job in the city and move into her own little apartment in the women's hotel."

"She hasn't even learned to read yet!" Clare cried. "I heard her laughing with James Terry about it. They both thought it was funny."

"Can't he read either?" Bonnie asked, astonished.

"Not very well. He told me that his uncle got rich building houses, and *he* doesn't know how to read. James wants to work for him and get rich, too, and have his own automobile."

"Why not?" Winnie said angrily. "Sometimes I wonder why we bother volunteering so much time at the neighborhood house when half the people who come to us want to get rich without learning any realistic way to accomplish it."

"We can't let ourselves be discouraged," Cousin Audra said. "We've had many successes."

"They probably were people who could have made it all by themselves," Winnie said.

"You mustn't give up," Cousin Audra said. "After all, Prohibition will be the law very soon now, and think what a difference that will make when the neighborhood house women don't have to struggle with drunken husbands who squander what little money they have on liquor."

"They'll find a way to get liquor," Sally said. "It'll just cost more than it does now. Things will be worse instead of better."

Cousin Audra stood up and folded the table cloth. "I refuse to look on the dark side. Things will get better."

Bonnie watched her leave the room and wondered

how Cousin Audra could remain optimistic in the face of all the things that were wrong with the world. Ever since the day Bonnie had seen the woman die under the streetcar, she had been struggling with unanswerable questions. Why did some people have terrible lives, while others, deserving or not, had everything? And why wouldn't some people even try to help themselves?

"Melba won't learn how to read," she said. "And she'll go right on lying about taking a bath when anyone who gets within a block of her can tell that she doesn't."

"And James Terry will get rich and marry her," Clare added bitterly. "And we'll be old maids with a whole box full of college degrees we can play Solitaire with."

A new boarder arrived, to take over the room Mr. Johnson had occupied. He was Mr. Reginald Reynolds, the manager of a small bank in the business district. Cousin Audra explained that he, like Mr. Nickerson, was a widower, and he was still in mourning.

Bonnie liked him the moment she saw him carrying a box of books upstairs.

"Can I help you?" she asked.

He looked down at her. "What? You help me? Young lady, these books weigh more than you do."

"The bookcase in your room is small," she said. "I think you'll need another."

"I always need another bookcase," he said. "And another. And another."

Bonnie smiled. He was a wonderful change after Mr. Johnson.

He was good company at dinner, too, and Mr. Younger's acid comments from the back parlor only amused him.

"That fellow's well read, isn't he?" he said to Bonnie, who sat across from him.

"He's learning Braille now, so he can go back to reading again."

"Good," Mr. Reynolds said. "He'll keep us on our toes."

Melba chose that moment to explode through the swinging door and say, "I'm turning off the gas under the meatballs unless somebody wants more. How about it, kids?"

No one did, so she disappeared again.

"Melba is one of Grandmother's projects," Clare explained.

"Clare!" Cousin Audra said sharply.

"That's all right, Mrs. Devereaux," Mr. Reynolds said. "I thought as much. It's kind of you to take on the responsibility."

"She does very good plain cooking," Mr. Nickerson said. "We have no complaints."

"That's what I like to hear," Mr. Reynolds said.

In the kitchen, Melba dumped all of the pots into the sink at one time, and sang out, " 'Oh, Johnny, Oh, Johnny, Oh.' "

Bonnie and Clare exchanged long-suffering glances.

On the evening of Bonnie's birthday, Mr. Younger tapped on his glass and asked her to sit down in the back parlor.

"I have something for you to honor the day," he said.

"You don't need to give me a gift," she said.

"On the contrary. I need to do this very much." He handed her a clumsily wrapped package.

She unwrapped it and found a book titled *Great Women in History*. "Thank you," she said. "I'm sure I'll enjoy it."

"Don't you dare put it on a shelf and ignore it," he said. "I'm going to ask you questions about it."

She laughed. "How do you know what's in it?"

"Miss Devereaux told me. She found it for me, too."

Bonnie opened the cover and saw her name printed inside, in large, shaky letters. "You wrote my name in it!" she exclaimed.

"All I am is blind, Bonnie," he said patiently. "I'm not stupid."

"Sorry," she said. "Of course. This is wonderful, and I will read it, I promise."

When she carried the book out of the room, Clare demanded to see it. She read the title and said, "Oh, pooh. I was hoping he would have given you something romantic."

"Why would he do that?"

"Because he has a case on you," Clare said. "Can't you tell? Everybody in the house probably knows about it."

Bonnie laughed. "You're too romantic," she said. "Mr. Younger is a busybody. He's trying to plan my future."

"Because he hopes he can share it," Clare declared.

"If Cousin Audra or your mother hear you talking like that, they won't like it," Bonnie warned her.

Clare only laughed.

Clare's father showed up again at the boarding house without warning at the end of May. He seemed quite relieved that Mr. Johnson no longer lived there, but he was irritated that someone else had taken the man's room.

"I don't like sleeping in that attic room," he told Cousin Audra in the hall. "It's too stuffy."

"I'm not offering it to you," she said. She eyed his suitcases coldly. "You can't stay here."

"I can stay with my daughter if I choose," he said.

Bonnie had been dusting the small desk in the cubbyhole under the stairs where the telephone was located, and she suspected that Cousin Audra didn't know she was there. But she stepped out into the hall anyway, and said, "Is there anything I can do for you before I go upstairs, Cousin Audra?"

Cousin Audra was clearly relieved at the interruption. "I'll go up with you," she said. She turned back to Mr. Harris. "Good-bye," she said. "I'll tell Sally you were here. If you have a message for her, you can mail it."

Mr. Harris drew a sharp breath. "I'm leaving for Canada in a week," he said. "I want to see my daughter."

"Write Sally and tell her that," Cousin Audra said. "Now you'll have to excuse me."

She held open the front door for him, and he left, slowly.

Bonnie let out the breath she had been holding when Cousin Audra shut the door. "Did you know he was coming?" she asked.

"No. I'll tell Sally as soon as she gets home. I hate to see Clare upset again by the man."

"What do you think he really wants?" Bonnie asked.

Cousin Audra sighed. "He always wants money. And I think he always wants someone to control. I doubt if he cares what happens to Clare. But he loves the idea of getting in everyone's way and refusing this and disclaiming that, just to show his power. Sally suffered a great deal when she was married to him."

Mr. Nickerson surprised them by abruptly announcing one evening at dinner that he planned to move in with his daughter. It was time he retired from the department store, and his daughter needed his help. She was, he said, in a delicate condition.

"She's pregnant again?" Winnie asked. "But she just had a baby awhile back."

A small silence greeted her remarks. The word *pregnant* was never used except by women speaking among themselves in a kitchen. Bonnie felt her face sting with a blush.

But Clare went on eating as if nothing unusual had occurred, although Bonnie suspected she was working hard to control a smirk. Of course, she was accustomed to the women's stand on controlling the size of families.

Mr. Nickerson changed the subject abruptly instead of answering, and Cousin Audra covered the awkward moment by asking Melba to bring in a fresh pitcher of water.

After dinner, Bonnie asked Cousin Audra how soon she would bring in a new boarder.

Cousin Audra gathered up the linen table cloth and napkins and said, "Perhaps I'll wait a while. I have something on my mind, but I'm not certain how it will turn out."

"What?" Bonnie asked as she moved the silver candlesticks to the side table.

"You'll see in good time," Cousin Audra said.

After that, Bonnie noticed that Cousin Audra and Mr. Partridge had several low-voiced conversations in the small library. Once Mr. Partridge came home from his law office early with papers for Cousin Audra to sign. Another time, late in the evening, the family's doctor came and spent an hour in the library with Mr. Partridge and Cousin Audra.

"Do you know what's going on?" Bonnie asked Clare.

Clare, bent over her desk and struggling with algebra, said, "No, but I'm sure that whatever it is, we won't like it. Bonnie, have you seen James talking to Melba lately?''

Bonnie shook her head. "No, not for a few days. He comes and does his work and then leaves again. Maybe Cousin Audra said something to him."

"Saying something to him wouldn't do any more good than saying something to Melba," Clare said. She slammed her algebra book shut. "I think Melba is sneaking out at night to see a man. And she made Grandmother give her Saturday nights off instead of Thursday nights. I heard them arguing about it."

"You should say something to someone, then," Bonnie said. "You know Cousin Audra won't allow her to go out with a man. She wouldn't even let her go for a walk with James."

Clare giggled. "She should have worried about what Melba could find to do without walking anywhere."

Bonnie thought over what Clare was hinting at. "Winnie read her one of the birth-control pamphlets," she said.

"She also read her the one about votes for women," Clare said. "I bet Melba and James got a big laugh out of that."

"You'd better tell Cousin Audra what you think," Bonnie said.

"That would be tattling," Clare said. She yawned and stretched. "I'm going to bed."

Tattling, Bonnie thought. Clare didn't hesitate a moment to tattle whenever it suited her purposes. She must want Melba to test Cousin Audra past her limits.

Dear Elena:

School will be out soon. I would be so happy if you came to visit us for a few weeks this summer. There

140

is an empty bedroom next to the nursery that you could use for as long as you like. If you want to come, then Cousin Audra will write to your parents and make all the arrangements with them.

Please come, Elena. We have so much to talk about, and I've missed you more than I can tell.

You asked about Mr. Younger. He is working hard at his studies, and he walks about the neighborhood a little now.

Wait until you see him. You will find him very interesting. Don't worry about his sarcastic ways. Before you come, I will warn him to be especially nice to you.

Please come, Elena!

Prohibition became law. No alcoholic beverages could be legally sold, but they were sold everywhere anyway. The boarders continued to go to the hotel for their after-dinner drinks every night, but now, Winnie said angrily, they drank them from cups instead of glasses, an attempt at deception that fooled no one.

"Men," Winnie said one Saturday during lunch when the women were alone in the dining room. "It's not possible to teach them much, is it?"

Sally sighed. "No. We have to find ways around them."

"You heard from Jacob?" Winnie asked.

"I got a letter this morning," Sally said. "He's coming back from Canada, and he wants Clare to go to Colorado with him. He has some sort of mining scheme set up."

"He can't take Clare!" Cousin Audra said.

Bonnie stole a glance at Clare. Her face was white as paper. "I won't go anywhere with him!" she cried. "I'd rather be dead."

"Don't worry about it," Cousin Audra said. "There is no possibility that a judge will give him custody of you. He's only trying to upset your mother."

"But why?" Clare demanded.

"Because he enjoys it," Winnie said. "Don't concern yourself. Nothing will happen."

But Bonnie noticed that Clare did not sleep well for several nights after that. She knew she was afraid.

A week after school let out for the summer, a new boarder arrived. This time it was a woman, and even more astonishing, it was the former wife of Mr. Johnson.

She arrived on a Sunday afternoon, brought to the house by Mr. Partridge, who had hired a taxicab for the occasion. Cousin Audra led the thin, pale woman into the front parlor and settled her on the sofa. Mrs. Johnson didn't speak, but her eyes filled with tears.

Bonnie and Clare stared and then hurried out to the hall to whisper together.

"Her head's been shaved." Clare fingered her long braid, as if she was afraid the same thing would happen to her.

"Did you see the scar on her forehead?" Bonnie whispered. "Did you see how terrible her clothes are?"

"She's supposed to be very rich," Clare whispered back. "I heard Mama and Winnie talking about it once. Mr. Partridge got her money back for her."

"He must have found a way to get her out of the insane asylum, too," Bonnie said.

"Should she be here with us, if she's crazy?" Clare asked. "I don't want someone who is really crazy staying here."

Bonnie thought of Elena, who would be coming to Seattle in another week. What would she think?

What would anyone think?

Mrs. Johnson, who was to be called Mrs. Carver now that she was divorcing Mr. Johnson, spent most of her days in her room. She came down for meals and sat huddled in a chair, never speaking, hardly eating. Winnie took her downtown and helped her choose a complete wardrobe; but the cheerful colors she now wore did nothing to help her appearance. She was thin and the stubble of hair that showed under the scarves Winnie tied around her head was growing in gray. The scar on her forehead remained an angry red.

Melba, crude as always, referred to her as the Dummy. "Does the Dummy want seconds on them eggs?" she would ask. "If the Dummy's going to have tea in her room at night, she has to bring the cup down herself," Melba declared. "I'm not going up for it again."

Bonnie and Clare were fascinated by Mrs. Carver— and half afraid of her. Neither of them had ever seen anyone before who had been put into a mental institution, and at first, they expected to see her become violent and begin throwing objects at people. But it became apparent very soon that Mrs. Carver was gentle and timid, and would harm no one.

"How long is she going to stay?" Clare asked her grandmother once while she and Bonnie were helping her cut roses for the table.

"As long as she wants," Cousin Audra said. "She pays for her room and board, which is more than Mr. Johnson always did."

"And my father, too," Clare said bitterly. "When will Mrs. Carver start talking?"

"When she's no longer afraid to have an opinion," Cousin Audra said sadly.

*   *   *

The day of Elena's arrival finally came. Winnie accompanied Bonnie to the train station to meet her, and they left nearly an hour early that Saturday afternoon.

"Remember when you arrived here last year and I kept you waiting?" Winnie said as they got off the streetcar. "I've never forgiven myself."

"There's a cafeteria inside," Bonnie said. "It's not very nice, but we could have a cup of tea there."

"Unless her train comes in early," Winnie said, striding along, her pleated skirt swinging.

The train station looked as depressing to Bonnie as it had the year before. It smelled just as bad, too. She directed Winnie toward the cafeteria, and suddenly stopped.

"What is it?" Winnie asked.

Bonnie stared. Ahead of her, sitting on a stool in the cafeteria, Melba leaned close to a fat man and laughed noisily. The man was the one who had offered Bonnie work in a hotel the summer before. A different man was behind the counter, so there was no one to rescue Melba from the man, who jostled her with his elbow and whispered in her ear, making her laugh again.

"That's Melba!" Winnie declared. "What is she doing here, when she should be shopping for dinner? Who is that man?"

"He's the same man who offered me a job in a hotel last summer when I was waiting for you," Bonnie said. "The man who worked at the counter then made him leave. The things he said made it sound as if the man is dangerous."

"A job in a hotel?" Winnie exclaimed, staring at Bonnie in shock. "He came up to you and offered you a job in a hotel?"

Bonnie nodded. "As a maid, yes."

"My god," Winnie said sharply. "He didn't want you

to be a maid! He's one of those people who preys on young girls who are new in town. They trap them into prostitution! Decent people have been trying to shut down those hotels for years, but they're owned by some of the richest men in town. This is an outrage!''

Winnie stalked into the cafeteria and grabbed the shoulder of the man who was talking to Melba. ''Get away from this girl instantly,'' she said in a cold and forceful voice. ''If you don't, I will have you arrested for attempted statutory rape. This girl is a minor and works for us, and if you have the intelligence of an earwig, you will get out of this train station just as fast as you can.''

The man stood up abruptly, glared first at Winnie and then at Bonnie. He showed no sign of recognition.

''I don't know who you think you are . . .'' he began.

''You don't want to find out, either,'' Winnie said. ''Melba, you are supposed to be shopping for dinner. Get up and get out of here. I'll see you back at the house, and then we'll discuss this.''

Melba's face turned an ugly, mottled red. She eased herself off the stool, twisted her lips into a sneer directly at Bonnie, and walked away, switching her hips arrogantly.

Bonnie was stunned. Prostitution? The man had been trying to lure her into that? She felt like bursting into tears.

''I don't want to have tea here,'' Winnie said indignantly. ''Come along. We'll wait on the platform for your friend.''

Bonnie followed, and her ears were ringing with shock. But what was Melba doing with that awful man?

She and Winnie sat side by side until Elena's train arrived, and the moment Bonnie saw her tall, dark-haired friend, she forgot about Melba and the man.

"You're here!" she cried as she hugged Elena hard enough to make her protest.

"For a whole month, Bonnie!" Elena said. "Who's this? Your cousin? Oh, Miss Winnie Devereaux. I'm so glad to meet you."

"Let's go home, young ladies," Winnie said. "I think we've had enough excitement for one day."

But more waited for them at the boarding house. Clare's father had arrived during their absence, and this time he was certain he had a reason to take Clare away with him.

12

⋆⊰⊱⋆

They found Cousin Audra in the front parlor with Clare's father. He didn't get to his feet when Winnie and the girls came in. Instead, he slouched a little in his chair, contemptuous, apparently at ease.

"Winnie?" he said. "Good. You're just in time. Run along, Bonnie. Take your friend away. This is no conversation for young ears."

Bonnie drew Elena partway up the stairs. "I've got to hear," she whispered to Elena.

"Good," she whispered back. "I don't like the look of that man."

"When I got here an hour ago," Mr. Harris told Winnie, "I found my beautiful daughter sitting out on the porch with that scoundrel Johnson's insane wife. I knew it was her. I was with him once when he went to the asylum to get a few papers signed—not that she was in any shape to sign anything. Let me tell you, that woman is dangerous. I won't have Clare in the same house with her, and since Audra insists that the lunatic is a permanent roomer here, then Clare goes with me."

"Where is Clare?" Winnie asked Cousin Audra.

147

"I sent her to the library to wait for Sally," Cousin Audra said.

"Are any of the boarders here?" Winnie asked quickly.

"Mr. Younger is out in the garden. Mrs. Carver is upstairs sleeping." Cousin Audra sounded exhausted.

"Good," Winnie said. "At least we don't have to drag in everybody else. Now listen, Harris, and listen carefully. Mrs. Carver has been released from the institution by a judge who said she is competent to live anywhere she wishes. There is nothing wrong with her. There never was anything wrong with her. You were correct in calling Johnson a scoundrel, because he had that poor woman committed so that he could steal her family's money. You do not have grounds to take Clare away from here, and she has said over and over that if you try, she will run away or kill herself. There is nothing more to say. Get out."

Elena stared at Bonnie. "This is the most exciting thing I ever heard," she whispered.

Bonnie, who had been embarrassed enough to regret her curiosity, relaxed. There were exciting aspects to living in a boarding house and being a part of the lives of so many people.

She heard the rustle of Cousin Audra's silk skirt. "I'm going to the telephone now," she said clearly. "If you haven't left the house by the time I reach it, I will call my lawyer, the one you don't like, and tell him you are here attempting to blackmail us."

Cousin Audra appeared in the hall below them. She opened the door to the little room under the stairs and stepped inside.

"Hello, operator?" Bonnie heard her say.

"She's really going to do it," Bonnie breathed.

"Wonderful!" Elena whispered.

Mr. Harris came out of the front parlor. "This isn't the end of it!" he shouted at Cousin Audra. "I'm Clare's father. I have an interest in everything that concerns her."

Cousin Audra appeared in the hall again. "I'm not dead yet," she said. "And you haven't seen my will. Perhaps I'm not leaving Sally and Clare anything at all. Have you considered that? Then you would have no claim on Clare's future expectations."

"You wouldn't dare cut her out," he said.

"We'll see what I dare to do," Cousin Audra said. "Close the door behind you."

The door slammed, rattling its glass panel.

Cousin Audra looked up at the girls sitting on the stairs. "Do you need help with your luggage, Elena?" she asked, smiling.

Elena bolted to her feet. "No, ma'am," she said. Her face was red. "I'll be going to my room now to unpack."

"Afterward, come down and we'll have lemonade and cookies on the porch," Cousin Audra said.

Bonnie watched her walk back in the front parlor. She is the mistress of everything, Bonnie thought admiringly. I'll learn how to be that way, too.

Elena was accepted immediately into the boarding house. The men enjoyed her quick laughter, even Mr. Younger, who pronounced her "Sharp as a hatpin."

"So sharp that you must sit in the other room and shout at me?" she called out to him through the door to the back parlor.

He laughed and banged his spoon on his glass. "Bonnie, are we having dessert tonight?"

"I'll bring it," Bonnie called back.

She excused herself from the table as Melba elbowed

her way into the room carrying a bowl of preserved peaches. Melba shot her a mean look and slammed the bowl down in the middle of the table. "Help yourselves," she said. She left the room without another word.

Bonnie brought small bowls in from the pantry and helped Cousin Audra serve the peaches. When she finally brought Mr. Younger's bowl in to him, he was tapping his fingers impatiently.

"I sense all sorts of undercurrents," he said. "It's more than just the arrival of your friend. What's going on?"

Bonnie told him quickly about Mr. Harris's appearance earlier in the day, and the unkind things he had said about Mrs. Carver. "But Cousin Audra sent him on his way," she said. "You know how she is."

"I know exactly," he said. He began laughing and then stopped. "That Harris fellow is trouble. I hope Clare isn't too upset."

"She doesn't know he was here," Bonnie said. "Cousin Audra asked me not to tell her."

"Good," he said. "Now go back to your guest. I hope you've made plans to show her the sights in Seattle soon."

"Beginning tomorrow," Bonnie said.

She heard him sigh as she left the room. It caused her a sharp pang of regret. Poor Mr. Younger. He would never see the sights of Seattle.

Winnie and Bonnie took Elena to the waterfront the next day, to show off the many ships waiting at the long docks for their cargo. They rode the elevator to the forty-second floor of the Smith Tower, the highest building west of the Mississippi, and frightened themselves with the view. Famished, they had a late lunch in the tea room at Frederick & Nelson's, and then bought chocolates in the candy store across the street.

"It's all wonderful," Elena told Bonnie that evening while they sat in Elena's room. "But you must come to see Los Angeles. You will be amazed."

She leaned forward and looked very sober. "Bonnie, Dad and I have a wonderful idea, and we hope you will think so, too."

"What?" Bonnie asked.

"Have you decided where you'll go to college?"

"Here, probably," Bonnie said.

"What if you went to college with me in Berkeley? That's where I'll be going."

Bonnie stared at her. "But I couldn't do that."

"Why not?" Elena demanded. "We could live in a woman's boarding house my mother knows about. What would you think of that?"

Leave Cousin Audra and Winnie? Leave the boarding house where she now felt at home? Move again?

She shook her head slowly. "I don't think I could do it," she said. "The university here is a fine one."

"Yes, but think of the adventure," Elena said. "We'd be on our own, the two of us. Doesn't that sound exciting?"

Goosebumps rose on Bonnie's arms. She had a family now, a safe place to live, and the ongoing adventures of the people in the house to keep her interested. Giving it up to move to a strange place didn't sound attractive.

"I don't know, Elena," she said. "I'll have to think about it."

"Promise you'll keep an open mind," Elena said, bouncing a little in her chair. "Promise you'll really consider it."

"Do you still want to be a teacher?" Bonnie asked.

"Certainly not," Elena said, laughing. "I'm going to study drama. I'll be an actress someday."

Bonnie Rose could only stare.

The next morning after breakfast, Mr. Younger clinked his spoon on his cup and when Bonnie responded, he asked her to sit down.

"What is it?" she asked.

"I'm concerned about the new boarder," he said. "Mrs. Carver's footsteps are uneven. And sometimes she makes a small sound, almost a whimper."

"She doesn't limp," Bonnie said, puzzled.

"I think she's trying very hard not to," he said. "Someone should see if she's all right."

As soon as Bonnie had a moment alone with Cousin Audra, she repeated what Mr. Younger had told her.

"I thought something might be wrong," Cousin Audra said. "But when I asked her, she shook her head."

"We'd better find out."

They climbed the stairs to Mrs. Carver's room and knocked on the door. After a moment, she opened it and seemed surprised to see Bonnie standing there with Cousin Audra. She smiled, though, and then cleared her throat. "Come in," she said softly.

Those were the first words Bonnie had heard her speak, but, hiding her surprise, she stepped into the room.

Cousin Audra said, "We're concerned about your foot, Mrs. Carver. Is there something we can do to help you?"

Mrs. Carver backed up a step and shook her head.

"We're afraid you might have hurt yourself," Cousin Audra said.

"I'm fine," Mrs. Carver said. She bit her lip almost

hard enough to draw blood. Then she said, "Please excuse me. I'm very tired."

Cousin Audra moved toward the door reluctantly. "If you're sure we can't help you . . ." she said slowly.

Mrs. Carver turned to look out her window.

Cousin Audra sighed. "All right, then. We'll see you later in the day." She walked out into the hall.

On impulse, Bonnie closed the door behind Cousin Audra. She was alone with Mrs. Carver now, and the woman whirled around, startled.

"This is a safe place," Bonnie said softly. "I was worried when I came here, but I learned that this is a very safe place. Everyone is valued. Everyone is taken care of. Would you please sit down and let me see your foot? I might be able to help."

Mrs. Carver stared at her, looked away, and then stared again. Finally she limped to the bed and sat down on the edge. Slowly, carefully, she removed her shoe and stocking.

Bonnie saw a deep, infected wound on the top of her foot. It looked as if something heavy had fallen on Mrs. Carver's foot, but the wound wasn't a fresh one.

Even though it hadn't healed, Bonnie was certain, from the amount of infection present, that it had existed for weeks, since before the woman left the asylum.

Bonnie controlled the expression on her face carefully. She didn't want Mrs. Carver to see how shocked she was.

"Once our hired man hurt his foot like this," she said quietly. "It didn't heal the way it should have, so he had to see the doctor in town. I think you need to see a doctor now."

"No." Mrs. Carver bent and began pulling her stocking back on.

Bonnie put out her hand and stopped her. "Don't do

that, please. You mustn't cover it until it's been cleaned. Please let Cousin Audra call a doctor for you."

"No doctor!" Mrs. Carver cried. "Never."

Bonnie understood suddenly. The poor woman had been mistreated in the asylum and didn't trust doctors any longer.

"Then let me help you," she said. "Let me wash your foot and dress it. I'll go to the doctor myself and ask for something to help you."

"No doctor!" Mrs. Carver said.

Bonnie groaned inwardly. "All right, then," she said. "No doctor. But you won't mind if I try to help, will you? I'll be very careful and do my best not to hurt you. I'll clean the wound and bandage your foot, and then you must stay in bed for a few days. I'll bring you books to read and come to see you often. Your foot will heal and you won't be in pain anymore."

She hoped that what she was telling the woman was the truth, but the wound was so serious that she was afraid she might not be able to help.

Mrs. Carver agreed finally to let Bonnie try to help her, so Bonnie ran off to get a basin full of hot water, strong yellow soap, and a rolled bandage. Mrs. Carver endured what must have been a very painful cleansing of the wound without a sound. When Bonnie was done, she made Mrs. Carver comfortable on her bed with her foot elevated on several extra pillows from the linen closet.

"I'll bring your lunch up here," she told Mrs. Carver as she was leaving the room. "Then tonight, after dinner, I'll change the bandage again."

Mrs. Carver nodded, and Bonnie closed the door.

Heavens, she thought as she stood in the hall holding the basin. What will I do if this doesn't work? She could lose her foot if it doesn't begin to heal soon.

Twice a day for the next week, Bonnie cleansed Mrs. Carver's wound and changed the bandage. At first, she could see no improvement. But on the sixth day, the edges of the wound seemed cleaner and the skin around it not so feverish. After ten days, Mrs. Carver came down for her meals again, and she was smiling.

"You worked a miracle," Cousin Audra told Bonnie in the pantry.

"I tied a paper strip to the Ornament Tree," Bonnie whispered. "I wasn't very sure of myself."

Cousin Audra laughed. "I think you had more to do with helping Mrs. Carver than the Ornament Tree did."

"Maybe," Bonnie said. Helping Mrs. Carver had satisfied something in her. She had conquered the fear that had left her almost helpless when Sally was ill.

Elena stayed a full month, and on the afternoon after she left, Bonnie took a book outside to read in the shade of the side porch. The day was humid, and rain had been threatening to fall.

Mr. Younger tapped his way out on the porch, carrying a large Braille book under his arm.

"Who's here? Is that you, Bonnie?"

She put her book down. "Yes, I'm here. What are you reading?"

He found his accustomed chair and sat down. "A very boring story about a man traveling through a mountain pass. He's taking forever doing it. What are you reading?"

"It's one of the books that belonged to Cousin Audra's husband," Bonnie said. "He was a doctor. Sometimes I look through his books. This one is about our digestive systems."

"Spare me the details," Mr. Younger said. "What would Miss Delaney at the academy think if she knew what you've chosen for summer reading?"

"She'd be pleased," Bonnie said. "We have science classes, and I'll have more this coming year."

"And then what?" he asked. "I heard your friend begging you to consider going to college with her in Berkeley. Do you think you might do that?"

"No," Bonnie said. "I like living here."

"You're a wise girl," he said. He sounded relieved.

They opened their books and read in companionable silence for an hour, until thunder startled them and sent them inside, away from the sudden storm.

On the last day of summer vacation, the house was empty most of the afternoon. Bonnie, who had gone downtown to Winnie's hairdresser to have her hair cut, came home first. The moment she unlocked and opened the front door, she sensed that someone was in the house.

"Hello? Who's here?" she called out.

There was no answer. Melba shopped at that time of day. Mr. Younger would not be home from his Braille class for another hour. Clare had gone to a matinee with Marietta and Cousin Audra. Winnie was at the neighborhood house, and Sally would be at the library until nearly dinner time. Even Mrs. Carver was out.

Bonnie left the front door open behind her. What was wrong? The hair on her arms stood up.

"Who's here?" she called out again. "I know someone's here."

A floorboard upstairs creaked. One of the boarders had come home, but something must be wrong, because no one had answered when she called out. She ran upstairs quickly.

At the end of the hall, Cousin Audra's bedroom door stood open, and inside her room, Clare's father was standing in front of her desk holding papers in one hand and Cousin Audra's pearls in the other.

"Get out of there!" Bonnie shouted. "You have no right to touch Cousin Audra's things."

He walked casually toward the hall, smiling. "Well, now, Bonnie, there's no point in becoming hysterical. Audra was holding some papers for me, and I need them now, and since she isn't home . . ."

"She would never keep papers for you," Bonnie said. "Put down the things you're holding and get out of this house."

"You're pretty sassy for a girl your age," he said. His smile faded. "I think you'd better mind your own business."

"I'm going to call the police," Bonnie said, and she whirled and ran downstairs to the telephone.

The operator took forever to come on the line.

"Number, please?" an unseen woman chirped.

"Please ring the police," Bonnie said. Her heart was beating so hard that the operator must hear it. "A man has broken into our house and he's taking things." She babbled the address.

Mr. Harris leaned over the banister. "What are you doing?" he shouted.

"The police are coming!" Bonnie cried. "The operator's getting them right now."

Mr. Harris swore and started down the stairs. He still held the sheaf of papers in one hand. The other hand came out of his pocket, empty.

When he reached the bottom step, Bonnie dropped the telephone and ran toward him. Before he could stop her, she snatched the papers from him and ran outside.

She expected him to follow her, but he didn't. She waited at the corner, breathless and frightened, and watched the house. He didn't come out.

The streetcar turned onto the street and rattled and clanged toward her. To her relief, Winnie got off.

"I found Mr. Harris in the house, stealing these papers and Cousin Audra's pearls!" Bonnie cried. "I called the police. He's still inside."

"What!" Winnie shouted. "That black-hearted scoundrel. What are these papers? Why, here's the copy of Audra's will! What's he up to?"

Winnie stormed across the street, with Bonnie running behind. "Don't go inside," Bonnie begged.

"I most certainly will!" Winnie declared and she climbed the steps. "You, Harris, get out of here!"

To Bonnie's great relief, a police automobile pulled up in front of the house then and two officers leaped out. She and Winnie explained the circumstances, and the officers marched inside. Moments later, they came back out, and one held Mr. Harris firmly by his collar.

"Caught him sneaking out the kitchen door," the officer said. "He says his wife and daughter live here."

"Nonsense!" Winnie cried. "He broke into the house to steal from us. Men like him will say anything. He's got Mrs. Devereaux's pearls in his pocket."

Mr. Harris protested, but the officers found the pearls and then dragged him to the auto and took him away.

Winnie looked on with satisfaction while she held the pearls tightly in her hand. "There was no point in telling them about Sally and Clare," she said. "It would only cloud the issue."

When Cousin Audra and Clare came home, Winnie told them what had happened, adding, "If it hadn't been for Bonnie, that thief would have made off with your will and your pearls and who knows what else. She's a hero, our Bonnie."

"You took a terrible chance," Cousin Audra told

Bonnie. "You shouldn't have challenged him. But I'm terribly proud of you."

"Will they keep him in jail forever?" Clare asked hopefully.

"No, unfortunately," Winnie said. "But he'll be there long enough to learn to stay out of our house."

But as things turned out, Mr. Harris was kept in jail for a different reason. He was accused of fraud in his dealings with Mr. Johnson and several other men in the city.

"I'm glad he's still in jail," Clare said one rainy October evening. "But he's my father, and the whole thing is embarrassing. Do you think the girls at school will find out?"

"Not unless you tell them," Bonnie said as she turned the pages of her chemistry book.

Mrs. Carver stuck her head in the door. "Girls, Mrs. Devereaux would like you to come down to her bedroom."

"Right away," Bonnie said. It pleased her to see Mrs. Carver taking part in the boarding house activities more and more each day.

When they reached Cousin Audra's bedroom, they found Winnie and Sally there already. Cousin Audra closed the door behind them.

"Sit down, girls," she said. "This is a serious matter."

"What?" Bonnie asked, mystified.

Cousin Audra sat and smoothed her skirt over her lap. "I'm sorry to tell you that Melba is pregnant. Now we must discover who the father is and see to it that he does the right thing."

"You should have read that pamphlet to her more than once," Clare said.

13

A week passed, while Cousin Audra and Winnie tried every way they knew to persuade tearful, defiant Melba to give them the name of the father of her unborn child. The boarders pretended ignorance of the entire matter, although the quality of the meals grew steadily worse until finally, Mr. Partridge observed one evening under his breath, dinner might as well have been cooked by the women.

"Melba acts as if the whole thing is our fault," Clare complained one morning while she braided her hair. "She sulks and throws pots around and sasses everybody. We didn't get her into this mess. She did it all herself."

Bonnie looked up from buttoning her school blouse. "That's what I was thinking."

"Maybe she doesn't even know who the father is," Clare speculated. She snapped a rubber band on the end of her braid.

"Or maybe it's James," Bonnie said.

Clare shook her head. "I don't think she's had anything to do with him for a long time. No, it's some man she met somewhere."

160

Or picked up at the train station, Bonnie thought. That awful fat man. Even thinking about him made her feel slightly ill.

At the end of the week, Cousin Audra's patience wore out. Clare reported to Bonnie at bedtime one night that Melba had been warned to give the man's name instantly or lose her job. Melba refused to give up the name, so Cousin Audra fired her.

"And Grandmother's buying her a one-way ticket to Portland on tomorrow morning's train, if you can believe it," Clare reported excitedly.

"Someone should go to the station with her to make certain she gets on the train," Bonnie said, remembering the man.

"Oh, Grandmother and Mama are both going. They're sending her to a place Mr. Younger's mother knows about, a home where she can live until her baby's born. That will teach her."

The next morning, a poor breakfast made up of milk, pale toast, and weak coffee waited for them. Melba was in the kitchen, but she refused to cook. Instead, she stood at the window staring out at the rain falling into the gloomy backyard.

How different we are, Bonnie thought with a pang she didn't understand. How different our paths are. How does it come about that one of us is sliding into disgrace and the other climbing into a secure future?

Stout Mrs. Klacker took over in the kitchen a few days later. Her cooking delighted everyone, and she also produced delicious cakes, cookies, puddings, and candy.

"Life doesn't get much better than this," Mr. Younger said one evening as he finished his orange upside-down cake.

"I suppose," Bonnie said vaguely. She was glancing

161

sideways at the newspaper folded up beside her, where she had seen an article about the college Elena would attend when she finished high school.

"What's on your mind tonight?" Mr. Younger asked. "You sound preoccupied."

She blinked and sat up straighter. "Sorry. My mind was wandering. Tell me about the class you'll be teaching at the Braille school after Christmas. Cousin Audra mentioned it before dinner."

"It's nothing important," he said, but she could tell that it was very important to him. "I'm glad to help out there when I can."

"I think it's exciting, you being a teacher," she said.

"I'm nothing of the kind," he said gruffly. "Now, where's the newspaper? I want to hear what horrors have been going on around the world."

Bonnie opened the paper and read all the headlines to him except the one about the college.

Lucky Elena, she thought. She's a year older than I, but still, she'll be on her own there. That must be the greatest adventure of all.

Dear Elena:

Thank you for sending the college information. The photographs of the campus are wonderful. If your family spends Christmas vacation in Berkeley, see what arrangements might be made for us to stay at the women's boarding house you mentioned. It's very kind of the doctor who owns it to offer to help me with my studies—if I actually do study medicine. I don't know yet what I'll decide, but if I join you in California, I'm quite certain that Cousin Audra would not give her permission for me to live in an apartment, even with you. Since the disaster with Melba, she has decided that all young women need to be protected from everything, including themselves!

Two nights before Christmas, Mr. Younger went to the symphony with Bonnie and Winnie. He pretended to be indifferent, but Bonnie knew how excited he was. He sat between them, and during *The Nutcracker Suite*, it seemed to her that he held his breath sometimes. He never stopped smiling, and near the end, he groped for her hand and squeezed it.

On the day before Christmas, his mother traveled by train to spend the holiday with him.

"I can't believe how much he's changed," she said late the first evening, while the women were having tea in the kitchen after the men had gone to bed. "I expected to find him much as I'd left him."

"I wrote you about the classes," Cousin Audra said.

"Yes, but I didn't think he'd be this enthusiastic. This place has been good for him."

"This place is good for everybody," Bonnie said, and her heart seemed to turn over. She was half-sick with guilt for not having told anyone that she might want to leave them next summer. But until she knew for certain that it was what she should do, she didn't want to alarm anyone.

A new strip of paper hung on the Ornament Tree, fluttering in the cold winter storms. "What shall I do?" she had printed.

Sometimes, when she lay awake at night in the bed her mother had slept in, she wished she could ask her mother for advice. What would you want me to do, Mama? she wondered. Ever since I helped Mrs. Carver, I've wondered if I might not be a doctor. Not a nurse, Mama. A doctor. What would you tell me?

On Christmas Eve, Mrs. Carver gave Bonnie a small silver charm shaped like a heart, with a note that read, "You mended mine."

The next morning, when Bonnie looked out into the side yard, she saw that the storm during the night had torn away her strip. She touched the charm, which she wore on a thin velvet ribbon around her neck, and smiled.

Mama, I'll make you proud, she thought.

After the new year, Bonnie received a thick letter from Elena, and Cousin Audra received not only a letter from Elena's mother but also one from the wife of the doctor who owned the women's boarding house.

"Are you serious about this move?" Cousin Audra asked Bonnie.

They were setting the table together, and Bonnie put another napkin in its place before she answered.

"Yes, I'm serious. I should have told you before, but I wasn't certain about where I could live or how it all might work out. But the letters are so encouraging. I believe Mama would want me to try this."

"You must know how much we would worry about you," Cousin Audra said. "And how we would miss you."

Bonnie raised her face to smile at Cousin Audra. "I'd be home every summer."

"Home," Cousin Audra said, and she smiled through her tears. "As long as you call this house home, then I know we won't lose you."

Bonnie's plans were announced at the dinner table, and the boarders toasted her with their coffee cups. Clare, surprised and more than a little indignant, raised her water glass and said, "I can't believe you kept all this a secret. Why do you want to go away? You've got everything here.''

Everyone waited for Bonnie's answer. Finally she said, ''Perhaps it's because I have everything here that I know I must reach a little farther.'' She hoped Mr. Younger, in the back parlor, listened and remembered what he had once told her.

But when she went in to read him the newspaper, she found the room empty. Mr. Younger had gone up to his room.

Each morning, a few minutes after the girls left for the academy, Mr. Younger tapped his way across the street and waited for the streetcar that would take him downtown, to the school where he taught. He would stand at the curb until he heard the streetcar, then step out when it came close enough and stopped. The motorman would always speak so that Mr. Younger could find the steps.

A few days after Bonnie's announcement, the girls left forty-five minutes earlier than usual because both were rehearsing for the school play. When they stepped out on the porch, they saw Mr. Younger down the block at the streetcar stop already, apparently waiting for the early car.

''Where's he going at this time of the morning?'' Clare wondered aloud. ''He certainly is eager to get to work, isn't he?''

''Wait,'' Bonnie said. Something cold touched her heart. She saw Mr. Younger standing at the curb, his head cocked, listening for the streetcar to come closer.

But something was wrong. Bonnie couldn't quite sort out what bothered her. Perhaps it was where Mr. Younger was standing, farther up the block than he usually did, closer to the intersection. The motorman on this run wouldn't know his ways. He might not even know that Mr. Younger wanted the streetcar to stop for him.

He might not know he was blind.

"Come on, Bonnie," Clare urged. "We need all the rehearsal we can get." She ran down the steps and turned in the opposite direction from the streetcar stop. She didn't look back.

Bonnie took a step and then stopped. The streetcar rattled down the street without slowing down. She was right. The motorman didn't know Mr. Younger wanted it to stop. Bonnie began running.

As the streetcar passed the intersection, Bonnie saw that the motorman was looking straight ahead. And at that moment, Mr. Younger stepped out on the tracks—and Bonnie remembered the woman who had killed herself in front of them.

"No, no!" she screamed. She rushed at Mr. Younger and knocked him backward off the tracks. He stumbled and fell, and she fell on her knees beside him.

"Are you crazy!" she screamed. "What were you trying to do!"

The streetcar stopped and the conductor leaped off. "What's going on?" he shouted. "What happened?"

Bonnie looked up at him and said, "He's blind. He was standing in the wrong place and didn't know how close you were."

The conductor helped Mr. Younger to his feet, found his cane, and pressed the handle into his hand. "You shouldn't stand out here alone, sir," he said. "Isn't there someone who can wait with you?"

Mr. Younger said nothing, but averted his head.

"I'll take care of him," Bonnie said. "I'll take care of everything."

Mr. Younger waited until the conductor climbed the steps and the streetcar continued on its way before he shook Bonnie's hand off his arm.

166

"Don't think I don't know what you tried to do," she said harshly. "What I don't understand is why you were doing it. How dare you?"

"Leave me alone," Mr. Younger said. He blundered off the curb and tapped his way across the street.

She ran after him. "You don't know where you are," she said. "You're twenty feet from where you usually cross, and you won't find the gate unless someone helps you."

"I'm sick of being helped!" he cried. "I hate it. I hate groping and stumbling and having to ask questions."

"I know," she said.

"You don't know. You can't know."

She bit her lip. "You're right. I don't know what it's like. I'm sorry I said something so stupid. But listen to me. You have friends here and a family in Portland. You have a job, people who need you, who look forward to your helping them every day. How can you even think of abandoning them?"

"You're abandoning your family," he said. He pulled away from her, but she took his arm again.

"You think I'm changing things in the boarding house by going away, and it won't ever be the same again. But look at all the changes that have happened since you and I arrived that day. You enjoyed knowing about them, even when you weren't a part of them. But now you're a part of everything, too. Now you have things to tell at dinnertime, even if you do yell them from the next room."

She guided him to the opposite curb, and then along the sidewalk to the porch. He kept his face stubbornly turned away from her.

"Listen, will you?" she demanded. "Can't you at least try to take my place when I'm away at school?

Mrs. Carver depends on me to make her laugh. I'll ask her to read to you in the evenings, and you can gain her confidence that way. She gets so discouraged. Can't you help Cousin Audra keep the men amused? Can't you cheer up Mr. Reynolds when he starts brooding about how his wife drowned and he couldn't save her? Don't you see the places where you're needed? Can't you take care of them until I get back?''

Cousin Audra came out on the porch. ''For pity's sake, what happened to you, Mr. Younger? You're all muddy.''

''He tripped,'' Bonnie said quickly.

''Come along, Mr. Younger,'' Cousin Audra said. ''Is your hand bleeding? I'll take care of it. Run along, Bonnie. You'll be late to school.''

''I'll see you this afternoon, Mr. Younger,'' Bonnie said loudly.

''Oh, certainly, certainly,'' he said angrily, waving her off. ''You needn't shout.''

She hurried away, but she looked back twice, until Cousin Audra had led him safely inside.

What possessed him to do such a thing? she wondered as she ran to school. A random thought struck her and she shook her head, as if to warn it off. How ridiculous. Mr. Younger couldn't care that way about her. She wouldn't be sixteen for weeks yet, and he was twenty-two. They were years apart.

But still, she thought. Still . . .

No. She shook her head again and sighed.

On a hot August morning, Bonnie packed her new trunk and watched James help his father load it into a truck.

''I still can't imagine why you're doing this,'' Clare said. She watched Bonnie brush her hair, now cut short in the latest style. ''You'll never get food better than what Mrs. Klacker cooks. And I should think a boarding house full of women students would be the most boring place in the world.''

"I'll miss you, too," Bonnie told her, laughing. She examined herself in the mirror on her wardrobe door and nodded at her reflection.

Clare's eyes filled with tears suddenly. "You're being mean," she said. "I really will miss you."

Bonnie turned around and stared. "Honestly? Do you mean it?"

Clare brushed her tears away angrily. "Don't lose your mind over it. Who will help me with math if you're not here?"

"Ask Mr. Younger," Bonnie said. "He can add a whole column of figures in his head. I heard him helping Mrs. Klacker with her kitchen accounts. Now. Are you sure I look all right?"

"You know you look nice," Clare said. "I wish I were coming to the station with you."

"Somebody's got to be here when the iceman comes so he can be paid," Bonnie said. "Cousin Audra and Winnie are going to the station with me, and Mrs. Carver is helping Sally at the library until it closes. Give me a hug now and I'll pretend you did it at the station."

Clare jumped up and hugged her for the first time since they met. "You've been my sister," she whispered. "I can hardly wait until you get back next summer."

It was time to leave. The taxicab waited below in the street, and the train would depart in an hour.

"Take care of everybody," Bonnie said, blinking back tears. She picked up her pocketbook and hurried downstairs.

"Ready?" Cousin Audra asked. "Do put your gloves on, child. No lady goes outdoors without her gloves."

"Sorry," Bonnie said, and she grinned when Winnie, who seldom wore gloves, winked at her.

They climbed into the taxicab and Cousin Audra told the driver where to take them. Bonnie looked back at the boarding house and smiled. The ice wagon was rolling around the corner. Rosamund, the horse, stopped in her accustomed place, and Clare strolled down the porch steps haughtily.

Some things would never change.

Late that night, a light summer wind stirred in the side yard, rattling the leaves on the old apple tree. A thin strip of white paper shook but did not pull loose.

Printed on it in crude, lop-sided letters was, "Bonnie, Bonnie, Bonnie."